FOR THE
GOOD
OF THE
CLAN
CORPORATE SHIFTERS

Lucille Yates

Kitty Hex Press

Dedication

To Jasmine
You brought out the best in this book. Thank you for
your perspective and help along the way.

Welcome to the Corporate Shifter world.

Nobody can run from their past...
Not even shifters.

This series is a collection of books sharing the same theme: corporate shifters.

In each story you will find a shifter who left their pack to join the corporate world, only to return and question if they made the right decision at all.

These books can be read in any order.

Chapter 1

Rachel

The familiar sounds of the sizzling grill and the clanking of plates brought a smile to my face. The Flint River Kitchen became my home away from home. I loved to bake and my Uncle Eddie, the owner, hired me to bake the desserts and the bread, so no one messed with me here unless they wanted an ear full from him. Unfortunately, it didn't give me enough status in the clan to stop the harassment of our leader, Tobias.

Nine years ago, Tobias took over as leader and alpha of the clan. The only person with the status to oppose him, his brother Oliver, left. Tobias wanted to follow the old traditions. According to the old rules, those next in line for succession must fight any siblings to prove their place. He wanted to fight Oliver to prove his dominance in the clan. Oliver didn't want to fight. He didn't want the responsibility of being Alpha and happily supported his brother. Tobias insisted on tradition. Oliver refused, and Tobias told him to leave. So, he left to give his brother the space to lead without worrying about him.

To be honest, Tobias did a good job. Until a month ago, when his temper and actions became unbearable. Before, he calmly settled a dispute with words and reason. Rarely did he resort to violence or insist on a battle between those involved. Now, he threw chairs and bellowed at any clan members who came to settle a feud.

The switch in attitude unsettled the entire clan. Tobias acted like he wanted to fight anyone who looked at him. He made it a point to proposition any woman in the pack that he deemed attractive. My home didn't feel safe. I opted to stay with one of my brothers for the last few weeks.

But here in the kitchen, my shoulders relaxed, kneading bread and crafting desserts for our patrons. This kitchen became my safe space. And as long as the kitchen had bread and the desserts listed on the menu were made, Uncle Eddie allowed me to make a dessert of my choice. He sold them as the 'Dessert Special'.

I loved making pastries, so most of the dessert specials contained a pastry element. Today, I planned to try baklava. Again. Making phyllo dough required patience and skill. It didn't always turn out well, so I stashed a few store-bought frozen sheets in the freezer. I came in early to start the phyllo dough. While it rested, I worked on what the diner needed.

"Rachel, what desserts are you making today?" Uncle Eddie peeked over my shoulder at the dough in my hands. "Bread isn't a dessert."

"We need bread sooner than we need dessert." I slapped the lump. "I'm making cheesecake and chocolate cake. We only have one slice of each. And the dessert special is baklava."

"What am I going to tell my customers that want dessert for breakfast?" His gruff voice held back a growl.

"To eat something healthier?" I looked up at the bear shifter. "You know your growl doesn't scare me."

"It used to." He laughed. "What am I going to do when you finally decide to go to culinary school?"

"What are you talking about?" I felt the heat rise under my collar. Only one person knew about my dream of being a pastry chef.

"I'm talking about the well-worn pamphlet for The Art Institute of Atlanta folded to the baking and pastry section. You want to go to their pastry school, right?"

My shoulders tensed. "I couldn't go even if I wanted to. It's just a fool's dream."

"Why couldn't you go?"

"Money for one. And it's not just tuition. It's

transportation and lodging. And I can't leave you high and dry."

"I did just fine without you for years, thank you very much. I opened this place up before you were born. Isn't that school located north of Atlanta?"

"Yes. Why?"

"I'm sure there's a shifter in the Atlanta area that wouldn't mind you crashing on his couch for a while."

I scoffed. "Yeah. I'm sure he would love that."

He might not love that, but I would. Oliver left when I was 16. We were always close, and I'd fallen in love with him years before. I hoped we were mates, but I wouldn't know until I turned 18. We probably weren't mates. And I wasn't ready to have my heart broken. Still, I talked to him every few weeks, too scared to ask to see him.

"He might. It's been a while since he's seen anyone from the clan. And I'm sure we can work out money for tuition. I might know someone near the school who would hire you."

"And what about papers? Very few people in our clan have the right paperwork to live and work in the human world."

Uncle Eddie rubbed my shoulders. "You would need to ask Oliver. I'm sure he'd help you out, since you'll be sleeping on his couch."

I didn't want to sleep on his couch. I wanted to sleep in his bed. If I worked up the courage to ask him for a place to stay, how would I handle it if we were not mates? He'd have to say yes in the first place. It didn't seem likely.

I swatted his hands away. "You presume too much."

"I just want what's best for you. You're my niece. And you'll never know if you don't ask."

I hung my head as he walked away. I placed the dough in a bowl to rise and moved on to making the chocolate cake. My shoulders didn't relax as I worked this time. Uncle Eddie got inside my head. Stupid Uncle Eddie. He didn't know anything. I had the money for tuition. I applied and received my acceptance letter last week. The thought of leaving for good froze me to the spot. I took a deep breath and basked in the smell of breakfast. I didn't have time to dwell on my dreams right now. Besides, could I really leave my family?

Yells filtered into the kitchen from the dining area. My advanced bear hearing picked up on the one voice I didn't want to hear. Tobias. I groaned and tiptoed to the door with a few of the other cooks. Tobias used to come to the diner a few times a week, but that stopped a month ago when his personality began to change.

"How dare you allow these people to eat here." His voice rang out.

"What are you talking about?" Uncle Eddie's gruff voice sounded smooth and flat.

"These...These gawkers come to stare at you and the rest of us. We aren't here for your amusement."

The only noise seemed to be Tobias's heavy breathing. A few chairs clattered to the floor. "Get them out of here." He growled after he spoke.

Gasps, followed by shushing, trickled around the dining room.

"No." Uncle Eddie's voice returned to its normal gruffness. "This is my place. Not yours. Not the clans. It's mine. I'm not asking anyone to leave but you."

I looked at everyone in the kitchen. They shared my same wide-eyed expression. No one challenged the Alpha, but my heart beat faster. Maybe biting back would help snap Tobias out of it.

"How dare you," Tobias whispered in a deep voice.

"I said you need to leave. You're scaring the customers. We can talk about this later." Uncle Eddie's voice didn't waver.

BAM!

Everyone in the kitchen jumped at the sound. We crowded around the door and peeked out. Tobias pulled his fist out of the hole he had made in the wall. Blood dripped down his hand. He made his way toward the door and pushed Uncle Eddie as he passed. My uncle didn't fall or step back at the touch.

"We'll discuss this later." Tobias slammed the door shut behind him.

No one made a sound for five minutes until Uncle Eddie let out an audible breath and sat on the stool behind him. And just like that, everyone went back to work. The cake batter went into the oven, and I started on the icing.

Tobias went too far. He almost exposed all of us. Sure, most of the humans in the diner knew about us, but the general public turned a blind eye to shifters.

With a flick of the switch on the mixer, a sigh escaped me. I didn't tell Oli about Tobias the last time we talked. I couldn't keep it from him any longer. The intervention from the elders wasn't working. Oli might be the clan's only hope.

Chapter 2

Oliver

I loosened my tie and greeted the receptionist at Landry & Caddel. Her nails and handbag matched the pink highlights in her gray hair. She smiled and waved as I walked past. The first floor of this four-story building held offices for the pharmaceutical sales reps that didn't want to work from home and conference rooms. Laboratories and various managers' offices filled the top three floors.

The sterile walk to my office on the first floor didn't take long. The best thing about the building was the pictures hanging on the walls. The receptionist picked them all out in an attempt to brighten up the place. She said all the prints came from a local artist in the Atlanta area.

I stopped in front of my favorite piece. A woman stood in front of a river with mountains in the distance. Her face looked behind her toward the river, where a lone bear sat. Its eyes stared right at me. It reminded me of home and of her.

It sat across from my office door, and at the right angle, I could see it through the small window in the door. I'd switched it with another picture years ago. Whenever I felt a little homesick, I'd peek at the print. But I couldn't go home. I made a promise all those years ago and planned to keep it.

I watched the sun sink lower in the sky. It felt nice to sit for a minute before ending my day. All the doctors I met with today were receptive to the new drug I promoted. Honestly, the drug sold itself. Science amazed me. Growing up, I never realized that a small pill could cure so many ailments. Not that my clan had any ailments. Shifters were immune to most diseases and often didn't have to worry about things like diabetes. And the new drug on the market helped just that, diabetes. It dramatically improved the healing rate of any injuries, reducing the need for amputations in diabetic patients.

I leaned back in my chair and swiveled toward my desk. Few of the other sales reps kept an office at the company, but I hated working from home. I preferred to keep it separate.

The phone blinked in front of me. I groaned. For the last week, that blinking light reminded me why I kept an office away from home.

With a sigh, I picked up the phone and listened to the messages. No one called this line before. All my clients, co-workers, and other medical professionals called my work cell. Somehow, someone from my old clan found this number and shared it with the others.

"Hey, Oliver," a shaky voice said. "It's Ivy. I hate to call and bother you. Your brother isn't doing so well. We'd appreciate a visit. He won't listen to us. I know people have been calling, but it's getting worse. He's openly growling at anyone who looks his way, even at humans when he's in town. He took a sledgehammer to Pine's porch, because he didn't like the color she painted it. Please help. Call me anytime you want to talk. My number is…"

I deleted the messages and moved to the next. Six voice mails in total. Thirty over the last week. All a variation of the first call, and each voice sounded more panicked than the previous. They were wasting their time and mine. I couldn't do anything. Tobias wouldn't listen to me.

Even if I went back, I wouldn't stay. Home didn't exist on the clan's land anymore. Not for me.

It ceased to be home the moment I left. I remember the look on my brother's face that day, all red from shouting, his eyes bulged out of his head, and his face pinched together. The sun bore down on both of us. Sweat dripped down my face from trying to get away from him.

I told him, "I'd rather leave than fight you."

"Are you a coward?"

"No. This is a fight I don't want to have. I will not challenge you."

"We are the heirs. We have to fight. The winner becomes the Alpha. It's tradition."

"To hell with tradition. You're the alpha. You can change the rules."

"Damnit, Oliver. I challenge you. Tomorrow at sunrise."

"Why?" I yelled. "I concede to you. That's the end."

"If you're not going to fight, then leave. I never want to see you here again."

Those words haunted me. I left during the night. The only things I missed were my brother and Rachel. Despite the four-year gap, Tobias and I were close before the fight. He looked out for me growing up. It seemed as if he knew what worried me before I could put it to words.

And Rachel was always there. The first time I met her, she sat crying in our living room because her brother, Coby, and Tobias wouldn't play with her. At the time, they didn't want me around either. She was three-years younger than me. I held out my hand to her and offered her my friendship. After that, I could never say no to her, except the once, when she asked me not to leave.

I ended up in Atlanta working odd jobs. Eventually, my natural charisma and gift of gab took me further than I thought possible. I landed a sales job at a pharmaceutical company. Eventually, I got a job at Landry & Caddel, the top pharmaceutical company in the Southeast.

The sound of my cell ringing brought me out of my thoughts.

The caller ID made me sigh. Rachel. We hadn't talked in a few weeks, but I knew why she called now. The same reason everyone did. I took a deep breath.

"What?" I wasn't in the mood.

"Oh? Did you forget your manners?" Rachel's brassey voice made me smile, even when angry. "Glad I caught you in a good mood."

"Ugh. It's been a rough few weeks."

"I thought you liked your job."

"I do. Are you calling to tell me the same thing as everyone else?"

"Depends. Is it about your brother?"

"Yes." My office phone rang again. I sent it straight to voicemail.

She sighed. "I didn't give anyone your number."

"Someone found my office number and shared it."

"It's really bad," she whispered. "He's acting really weird."

"He's always weird."

"You think that, but this is…troubling."

"I don't know what y'all think I can do to help." He had never listened to me before. I couldn't imagine having any influence over him now.

"Anything. He won't listen to the elders. Everyone is scared." Her voice quivered. "There isn't a woman who he hasn't groped."

"Even Myrtle?"

"Even Myrtle. She stabbed him with her fork. She said she might be a hundred but wasn't about to be assaulted by some young buck."

I shook my head and laughed. Myrtle didn't back down from anyone.

"He came to the diner yesterday for the first time in weeks."

"I thought he came by all the time."

She paused, but I heard her breathing. "He did. But that stopped when he changed. He punched a hole in the diner's wall. I thought he was going to hit Uncle Eddie."

"Has he hit anyone?"

The line fell silent. I instinctively held my breath.

"Rachel?" I whispered.

"I'm here."

"Has he actually hit anyone?"

"Yeah. He has."

"Did they deserve it?"

"No. I don't know what the others have told you, but Tobias is out of control. We will take any help we can get. Please, Oliver."

I closed my eyes. "Did he touch you?" My heart pounded. I had to know. Silence filled the other side. "Where are you right now?"

"I'm sitting in the big oak tree with all the

initials." Her soft voice floated into my ear. "Please think about it. It's getting out of hand. They don't know what to do beyond drastic measures."

"I thought I was the drastic measure." I tried to crack a joke, but I couldn't even smile when I said it.

"You're the step before drastic. I'll talk to you tomorrow. Please think about it."

She hung up before I could answer.

I sighed. Drastic measures, huh? The clan had a group of four elders at all times. Each one was voted in by the clan and approved by the alpha. No one under sixty could be nominated. The group acted as advisors to the alpha, sharing their wisdom and performing ceremonies if needed. And if the behavior of the alpha negatively affected the clan, they could put down the current alpha and give the position to the next in line. They called it taking drastic measures. It must be bad to consider taking out the alpha. No one talked about whether the elders had killed an alpha in the past. I also never asked. As the next in line, I didn't like it.

As kids, I followed Tobias around like you'd expect from a younger brother. He took me fishing and hunting. He even included me in most of his plans with his friends. When our mom died, our dad was busy with clan responsibility, so Tobias stepped up and took care of me. I'm sure when I refused to fight him that day, it felt like a slap in the face. I stood by my choice. A fight wouldn't make his position more legitimate.

No, he didn't listen to me then. He won't listen to me now. But I itched to try, if only for Rachel's sake. Her unspoken yes when I asked if he's touched her made me stick to my stomach. As much as Tobias liked to follow the old rules, he always treated the pack with respect, no matter what. Something had happened to him. How on earth was I supposed to help?

Chapter 3

Rachel

A cool fall breeze blew through my short hair as I rubbed my thumb over the set of initials I wished were mine at the top of the old oak tree. A heart surrounded the initials OS + RW. I told myself they stood for Oliver Stallard and Rachel West. I didn't know how long ago they were carved. I climbed the tree while tipsy the night I turned twenty-one. The tree made me feel safe. And that one spot gave me a spark of hope.

I climbed down and walked back to my house, furious at Oliver's lack of concern regarding his brother and the clan. My heart ached. I couldn't deny it. His lack of concern for me made me angrier than his attitude toward the clan.

I walked through the dark house and ended up on the floor of my bedroom. It didn't give me the comfort it once did. Even on the edge of the pack grounds, I didn't feel safe. Tobias prowled the grounds at odd intervals. His distorted-looking face sent chills up my spine, triggering my flight instinct.

I never knew I had a flight instinct. When push came to shove, I always fought. The black bear inside me liked a good scuffle, but something about the alpha scared me.

Tobias never scared me before. Even when he pushed to fight Oli, I didn't cower.

I hauled myself off the floor and pulled a bag out of the closet. I sent a quick text to my brother, "I'm going for help."

~

Oliver

After the day I had, I deserved a drink. I didn't plan to drop by my favorite bar, but I drove there on autopilot. The sounds of the busy bar washed over me when I walked through the door of the Sarcastic Squirrel Café. The local café served as a coffee shop in the morning and switched to a bar at night. You could order alcohol starting at 11:30 a.m.

I liked how the owners kept large trees around the place. They looked like support beams climbing into the upper floors.

"Oliver," Salma, the owner, said. "Good to see you."

I looked up at Salma. I always looked up at her. She stood a good five inches taller than me. Her straight, black bob and pale skin accentuated her red lips. Apparently, her entire family was over six feet and all squirrel shifters.

"You, too." I sat at the bar. "What's new on tap?"

"We only have one new one today. It's a barley wine from Reformation Brewery. "

"I'll give it a shot."

"That's what I like about you. You'll give anything a try."

She brought over the pint and leaned in. "You look more stressed than usual. What's bothering you?"

"Just hometown stuff."

"Really? I thought they didn't talk to you."

"They usually don't. Apparently, my brother is causing problems."

"What does that have to do with you?"

I held her gaze. "He's the alpha," I said, just loud enough for her to hear.

Her ears twitched. I met Salma all those years ago when I left the Flint River Clan. The clan didn't play nice with the government, and I had no legal paperwork to work outside of pack land. Shifters were an unspoken group the government did not officially recognize. Salma not only runs this establishment;

she also helps obtain papers for wayward shifters.

She left her own clan years ago when she wanted to do more than hide from the world. The smaller shifters tended to either completely hide away or infiltrate into society as a whole. No one looks twice at a squirrel. And the trees inside the place were a great place for her to scamper around when the weather turned sour.

Her wife, Zola, walked by us and smiled up at Salma. The short, curvy human doted on her wife. She was soft-spoken but always friendly with the customers. The two of them clearly loved each other and openly expressed that with small touches and kisses while they worked. Salma winked at Zola, then turned to watch her lady walk away.

"You never miss a chance to look at her ass."

"Damn right. You'd better miss all the chances." She smiled at me. "I may be small when I shift, but I'm bigger than you as a human."

I raised my hands. "You're not someone I would ever cross."

"So, what are you going to do?"

"I don't know. He's not acting like himself. He's punching holes in walls and groping people."

"He feel up that girl you like?"

I raised my eyebrow at her, unwilling to acknowledge the truth.

"You know, that woman you talk about all the time but are unwilling to go back and see because you are afraid she's not your mate?"

"How are you so observant?" I sighed. "I think he touched her. She didn't answer me when I asked."

"Tough break. You may need to check out the situation after all. How bad do you think it is?"

I took a large gulp of beer. "I've been getting calls on my office phone for about two weeks from several members. They are desperate."

"And what can you do?"

"I honestly don't know."

She patted my head. "If I come up with a good idea, I'll let you know. For now, just take it easy."

The crowd thinned as closing time approached. I didn't want to leave just yet. My home felt like an empty shell, furnished yet lacking. I really missed having close shifter friends, and Salma and her wife were as close as I'd gotten after all these years. It's not something I admitted to myself unless I consumed alcohol.

The two women closed up the bar and listened as I talked about the pack and my brother. It's nothing new for Salma. She had heard parts of my story before. Today it felt different.

"I remember when Tobias and I would go fishing. One time my pole broke, and I begged him to let me use his. He decided we needed to learn how to catch them with our bare hands. So, we waded out into the water in just our shorts, trying to grab a fish." I felt more sober after the third glass of water and the tenth Tobias story. "That was the day Rachel shifted for the first time."

Zola put her hand on mine. "Tell me about it."

"She came running over the hill and straight into the water. We didn't recognize her at first. Not until we smelled her. Tobias just splashed her and told her to stop scaring the fish. I patted her head and congratulated her. She paddled around the lake, then dove headfirst into the water. When she came up, she had a fish in her mouth. She walked it on shore and dropped it onto Tobias's lap. She told me later that as soon as she shifted, I was the first person she went to find." I put my head in my hands.

Salma rubbed my head. "It will be okay."

"She's my best friend. I can't just not help her."

Did the clan really want me back? Would I need to leave again if I didn't fight Tobias? I also didn't want him to die needlessly. I knew what I needed to do, but I really hated it.

Zola pushed me out the door after I had sobered up a bit more. She might be short, but her strength always surprised me. How could a human push me around like that?

"I don't really understand your situation," she said in her soft voice at the end of the block, "but I do know that you don't have to stick to a decision you made a decade ago. People, shifters, we all change. What matters are our actions."

"It's complicated."

"I never said it wasn't." She patted me on the back. "You won't know if this is a pivotal moment until it passes you by. If you need help, you know Salma and I will do what we can. I also see the look in your eyes when you bring up a certain someone. Maybe this is your pivotal moment."

Chapter 4

Oliver

I thanked my shifter metabolism the next day as I sat at my desk organizing my to-do list for the day. Last week, my boss invited me to a private meeting scheduled for today. I stretched when my boss's boss poked his head in the door.

"Oliver Stallard. Just the man I wanted to see." Arthur Landry, one half of Landry & Caddel, smiled at me. He focused on the sales portion, while his partner, Caddel, focused on the research. Wrinkles surrounded his eyes when he grinned. The man never lost a sale because of his charisma. I rarely heard a negative word about him.

"Are you ready for this meeting? It's going to be a game changer." He dazzled me with the smile that charmed all his clients.

"Sure am. I'll walk with you, Mr. Landry."

He walked with me down the hall. I buttoned the top button of my jacket. I took pride in wearing high-quality suits, but Mr. Landry's perfectly tailored ensemble reminded me of how much further I stood from the top.

"Call me Arthur," he said. "You know, Oliver, you have the best sales in this office."

"The medicine sells itself."

"Nonsense. You're the perfect addition to this project. We only have one person on it right now, but she's going to need help. This is going to be big. I can feel it." He patted my shoulder before entering the room before me.

The conference room looked as sterile as the hallways. The only color came from the few framed photos of the Atlanta skyline, which hung on the walls. Arthur sat at the head of the table. My direct boss, Mac Peterson, sat next to him. Mac gave me a big wink when I sat next to him.

Mac and I had roughly the same build, but he had thick blonde hair and a good ten years on me. On first impression, he seemed to be an upstanding guy. Though, after working for him these last few years, I'd learned he tended to cut corners.

One of the scientists from upstairs sat on the other side of Arthur, and my only real competition in sales stood in front of the projector with a

PowerPoint presentation primed and ready.

Cindy Deak stole the show wherever she went. Most men's eyes followed her short, thin figure and her curly red hair. Her southern accent didn't sound strong until someone made her angry. I'd only seen her angry once and once was enough. All her competitors underestimated her until they looked at her numbers. I couldn't deny it; I'd done the same thing. I imagined we'd end up with a tumultuous rivalry, but she subscribed to the philosophy of killing with kindness. In the end, I had to give up the one-sided rivalry, and we became friends.

Cindy wore a bright blue skirt suit with a yellow blouse. The bright colors were her signature and matched the smile she gave everyone. Today, her smile didn't quite reach her eyes, and she shifted from foot to foot in front of the group.

"Everyone," Arthur said, "before we get started, what we are about to discuss today is confidential. You are not to discuss any of it outside of this room or with anyone apart from the people before you today. Alright, Cindy, let's get started."

She nodded her head and clicked the remote in her hand, advancing the slide on the screen.

"As you all know, we've released a new supplement onto the market called Brawn-tality. It helps people increase their strength by encouraging repairs to the muscle. It's a big hit with males ages 18 to 45. A few months ago, I was asked to expand that market."

She advanced the slide to show a photo of a pack of wolves. "I have been tasked with promoting this supplement to the shifter community."

I stared at her, then looked over at the others. Mac's eyes looked like plates. Arthur and the scientist smirked at our reactions.

"What?" Mac stammered. "Shifters are not real. It's just a legend, like bigfoot."

"They are very real, Mac." Arthur laughed. "And it's time to pull them into our market."

My phone dinged. "Sorry, let me turn off the notifications."

My hands felt sweaty, holding my phone. Shit. How could this happen? Who came up with the plan to market to shifters? I didn't know if this project was more dangerous for the company or for the shifters. Either way, I'd need proof. I hit a few buttons and placed it on the table. This could be a problem.

"Yes. Shifters are real. I have contacted two organizations. One refers to themselves as a pack, the other as a clan. Each has a variety of shifters." Cindy advanced the slide to a graph.

"They can really shift into different animals? Like one person can be whatever animal they want?" Mac's leg bobbed up and down under the table.

"No. A shifter is born able to shift into one animal and not of their choosing. It would be the same as the animal their parents shift into." The scientist said.

"And why would they want to use Brawn-tality?"

I asked.

Cindy gave me a weak smile. "They are strong, but this could make them stronger and heal faster. It's perfect for a sick shifter or as a preventative measure against 'Shifter's Disease'."

"Shifter's Disease…" It came out of my mouth before I could stop it. Those two words sent cold shivers down my spine. When I was ten, my mom passed away from it. Just hearing the words brought memories of her laying close to death. It worked like a fast-moving cancer. It wasn't contagious, but it also had no cure.

"No one knows exactly what it is, only that when a shifter gets it, they die within days," Cindy explained.

"And our product can really prevent it?" Mac asked.

"We don't know that for sure. It might. We don't have the funding to test it, but it can't hurt." Arthur smiled so widely the lights glinted off his teeth.

"Have we done any testing on how it affects shifters?" I asked. No one answered the question. I focused on controlling my breathing and my expression. These people knew about shifters for an undisclosed period of time. They knew about 'Shifter's Disease', yet they've done nothing to help.

"The two groups have taken to the supplement well and are purchasing more from the local stores." Cindy bit her lip. "The plan is for me to continue working with groups in the western part of the state and for Oliver to contact groups in North Georgia."

I leaned forward. "Why are they trusting you? I heard they don't trust outsiders and have a heightened sense of smell."

Most shifter groups interacted with humans as a necessity. We worked and went to school with humans, but our parents taught us to be wary. We could be friends, but never fully trust them. And to never invite them to the clan's territory.

Our real friends, they taught us, came from our clan and from the other shifter groups within driving distance. Growing up, The Flint River Clan had get-togethers with neighboring groups. I rarely met a human amongst them.

"Wonderful question." Arthur turned to the scientist. "Dr. Thorne?"

Dr. Thorne smirked and shook his long hair out of his face. "As part of a different project, we developed a solution taken orally that changes a human's scent to that of a shifter. Though, from our research, the scent created isn't that of a specific animal, only a general shifter smell. It lasts roughly 48 hours, depending on the person."

I didn't know what to say. Everyone else smiled at the doctor. Only Cindy looked nervous.

"For me, the product lasts about 40 hours." Cindy gave me a forced smile. "When they ask me what kind of shifter I am, I dodge the question as best I can."

"Are there any side effects?" Mac asked.

"I get itchy sometimes and dry mouth. But it's nothing compared to the effects of braw...other medicines I've taken." Her face flushed red.

"Oliver, you will be a perfect fit to introduce this product to shifters in North Georgia. Not only do you have an excellent sales record, but you aren't intimidating." Arthur pushed a file toward me.

"Excuse me?" His statement caught me off guard. I'd been told hundreds of times I wasn't a scary person, but this was the first time I'd ever felt insulted. My stoic schooled expression broke.

"Not to say you aren't manly," he backpedaled. "But Cindy mentioned the groups tend to work in a hierarchy. Reaching out to a clan will be easier for individuals with more charm than dominance."

Dr. Thorne stood. "I have another meeting to attend. Thank you for your time. I look forward to your updates."

Arthur stood as well. "Let's end this here. Oliver, look over the file. Next week, I want you to start on this project. I'm sure Cindy will answer any questions you have."

Arthur and Mac left after the scientist. Cindy put away her laptop and cables without a word.

"What's worrying you?" I crossed my arms and leaned against the table.

"Nothing." She smiled. "Everything is great."

I narrowed my eyes. "What kind of side effects do the shifters have when taking Brawn-tility?"

She wouldn't look at me. "None. I don't know

what you're talking about."

I gently wrapped my hand around her upper arm. "Let's go somewhere else to talk."

"What are you doing?" She squirmed as I walked her out of the room into the hall.

"That supplement. Does it cause irritability and increased violence in shifters?"

"Why would you ask that?" she whispered.

"Well…?"

"Only if they take too much."

"What were the names of the packs you are visiting?"

"Granite Bear Pack and Flint River Clan."

I stared down at her with wide eyes as I opened the door to my office and led her inside. The aroma in my office stopped me in the doorway. Peaches and vanilla took me out of my body. I looked up to see a woman standing at my desk. Dark brown pixie-cut hair, tiny pink lips, and dark blue eyes demanded my attention. My eyes roamed over her small tits, wide hips, and long, plump legs. I bet she could wrap those legs around me and never let go. Dark blue eyes looked into mine. My wolf perked up. The word 'mate' echoed in my mind.

"Hey, Oli," she said in her husky voice.

"Rachel."

"You can let me go now." Cindy pulled her arm out of my hand. "I see you know someone from Flint River."

Chapter 5

Rachel

My first thought when I saw him again after all these years was, 'damn'. He stood in the doorway of his office and stared me down with those rich, dark eyes of his. He still kept his dark brown hair short and the beard he couldn't quite grow when we were teens filled in nicely and looked inviting. I never thought I'd like a man in a suit, but he proved me wrong. It fit him perfectly across his broad shoulders, tapered down to his waist. I wanted to see what he looked like with his shirt unbuttoned.

Rage followed those thirsty thoughts. He had his hand on the arm of a tiny woman in heels. That woman, the one who interested Tobias. How did he know her? Why did it make me so angry?

My bear chuckled. She sniffed the air, calling my attention to the wave of sandalwood and cardamom that accompanied Oliver. I swallowed. All my dreams of Oliver Stallard being my mate landed in my lap, and he had his hands on some other woman.

"Hey, Oli."

"Rachel." He hadn't moved since he entered his office.

"You can let me go now." The woman pulled her arm out of my hand. "I see you know someone from Flint River."

"So, you're the reason they are having a hard time with the alpha?" Oli's attention stayed on me.

"Yes," she mumbled. "Arthur and Dr. Thorne don't care. They want to keep going."

He broke eye contact and glanced at her. "Don't worry about them. I'll take care of it."

"Okay." She rushed out the door behind him and closed it.

"I came here to bring you home, but it seems like there's more going on here than I realized. Are you sabotaging your own family?" I stuck my hands on my hips. Others suspected that woman to be behind Tobias's change, but this confirmed it.

He pulled a phone out of his breast pocket and punched a few buttons before putting it back. "My boss pulled me onto the project today. I had no idea this company knew about shifters."

"What exactly is happening? And how do you

know that woman?" The longer I stood there amongst his scent, the harder it became to act rationally.

"What woman?" His face scrunched up for a second, and he looked around the room.

I growled and walked toward him. "What woman? The one that just left!"

"What? Oh. Cindy? She's a…co-worker."

"Why have I seen her on Flint River land?" I stood in front of him, hands shaking and blood boiling. "What did she do to the alpha?"

He obviously didn't feel the same way I did about the clan, but he could fake a little remorse. His hand cupped my cheek. It startled me. Before I could stop him, he pulled me into a hug. I could hear him sniff me. He rubbed his face on my neck. The feel of his beard on my neck made me weak in the knees.

I gave in and wrapped my arms around him. My face burrowed into his shoulder as I inhaled the scent that called to my bear and me. The anger inside of me melted away. It left me with pure need. My fingers pulled at his jacket, and I rubbed my body against him unconsciously. His body mimicked mine, rubbing back, his hands roamed under my tank top, and his cock hardened against me with every move. I slid my hand into his dark hair, jerked his head to the side, and licked up his neck to his ear. He hissed and moaned, then he pulled my hands away from his body.

"We can't. Not here." He kissed my hands.

"Sure, we can." I nibbled at his fingers in my

hand.

"Rachel. I'm at work." He looked down at the floor.

"Is work that important?"

He sighed and looked up. "It is when it's the key to helping Tobias."

"You said you couldn't help him."

"I did. That was before I knew about their new project. Besides, you came here to take me back. Didn't you?"

"I did," I whispered. "But I don't want to go back now."

His hand caressed my cheek. "You don't have to, but you can't stay here. Let me pull some files together, and we can talk after work."

"I can stay here while you work."

"You most definitely cannot stay here. I'm barely holding onto any rational thought at the moment." He dipped his head down and lightly kissed me. He pulled out his keys and handed me one from the ring. "Here. This is the key to my place. Do you have the address?"

"Yeah."

"Go there. We can talk when I get off and come up with a plan."

The key felt warm in my hand. I could barely remember what we needed to plan, but he was right. I needed to clear my head. The mate pull overwhelmed my every thought. He turned me toward the door and kissed the back of my neck.

"I'll walk you to the front."

My head pounded as I walked beside him down the hall. On the way in, all I could think about was how boring the company looked, but now I had to concentrate on not pulling him into an open room.

At the building's entrance, he shook my hand. "Thank you for visiting Ms. West. Please, don't hesitate to call me with any issues." He winked and left me standing in the entryway.

I really needed a cold shower. Maybe a drink.

~

Oliver

After closing my office door, I adjusted my semi-hard dick. I needed to think about anything else, but Rachel's smell permeated the room. I leaned against the door. I sent her to my home. Her scent would be there as well. I wouldn't be able to walk around my house without a stiff dick for weeks after she leaves.

She doesn't have to leave, my wolf said.

I pushed off the door and made my way to my desk. She would leave. I couldn't go back home, not to live. She had her own life there. How could I ask her to leave everything behind for me? She had her own job and a house. Her dreams didn't revolve around me. She couldn't leave her family, especially since her family was sane, unlike my brother.

Shit. I'd forgotten about Tobias. I pulled up the company's files. There had to be something here about Brawn-tality. The company could spare me for a few days. And today, being Friday, gave me more time. I'd need to cancel all my appointments and ask for a few days off. Turned out I had the key to help Tobias after all.

Chapter 6

Rachel

Oliver lived in a small subdivision right next to a nature preserve. His backyard backed up to it, and I knew he used it to his advantage to shift and run through there. Not shifting hurts the animal, just as shifting too much hurts the human.

A bright yellow door greeted me when I pulled up to his brick home. Juniper and dark maroon rhododendron bushes lined the front of the house. A lovely dogwood whose leaves had turned red and orange, stood on the right side of his yard.

Inside, the home smelled like him, much to my delight. I checked out each room of the three-bedroom ranch. My favorite room was obviously his kitchen. The large open layout opened into the dining room. The light green walls covered both the kitchen and dining room. It looks perfect next to the rustic, yet sturdy looking farmhouse style kitchen table. The marble countertops wrapped around the kitchen and complemented the green and brown glass backsplash. It had copious amounts of storage between the cabinets and the island. He even had my dream refrigerator. The only thing that could make it better is if it had a double oven.

Eight-foot privacy fences lined the sides of his backyard. A line of what looked like ribbon grass grew next to the fence. Next to the house on the left side of the patio sat a lovely succulent garden. The right side had rose bushes.

As the property backed up to the preserve, he didn't include a visible fence to the rear. Near the tree line stood a lonely peach tree, whose leaves looked ready to shed. I wondered how often he shifted to run through the preserve. Was it really safe?

After opening each door and cabinet, I returned to his bedroom. He picked out dark wood furniture for this room. The walls were a light gray. Instead of an accent wall, he opted for accent curtains in yellow. I preferred dark blackout curtains, but the yellow looked amazing with the rest of the decor. I never realized he had such a great sense of style. After peeking into his half-filled walk-in closet, I sank into his queen-sized bed and stuck my face into his pillows. Oh, so good. I didn't even care if he'd know

I'd been on his bed or all around his house.

When we were kids, we would have sleepovers at each other's houses. It alternated depending on whose parents went on a date. Either Oli or I gave up our bed to the other's brother. We slept together on a pallet made of soft blankets on the floor. Oli would hold my hand until I fell asleep. When he turned thirteen, we stopped sleeping on a pallet together.

After twenty minutes of rolling in his scent, I knew I couldn't stay here much longer. I kept picturing Oli naked, crawling on top of me, and licking me all over. As much as I'd like to masturbate to the new and improved image of Oliver in my head, I couldn't bring myself to do so. At least, not before I had the chance to finish what we started in his office. Well, almost started.

I scurried off the bed. I had to go somewhere for a few hours before my entire body vibrated with need for him. Earlier, a flyer on his fridge caught my attention when I explored the house. The logo of a squirrel with coffee in one hand and a shot in the other made me laugh. The Sarcastic Squirrel Café sounded like a great place to kill some time.

~

Oliver

Each new file I pulled up on Brawn-tality caused a new level of worry. The difference between the creator's and the public information documentation made my blood boil. How could anyone be comfortable lying about a product to this extent?

After a few hours of digging, I walked over to Cindy's office. I knocked on her open door and entered before she could speak. With the door closed, I sat across from her with a frown.

"What?" she asked.

"What exactly do you know about Brawn-tality?"

She took a deep breath. "It's a supplement designed to rebuild muscle quickly after a workout and decrease inflammation. It contains DHEA, Beta-Alanine, and Creatine. All are listed as supplements, not regulated by the FDA. The scientific drug name is vipotolone."

"What's the dosage for shifters?"

"Dr. Thorne said they have faster metabolisms and can take up to double the normal dose as humans."

I rubbed my face. "Did they tell you it contains a low amount of anabolic steroids?"

"What? No!" She leaned forward, her mouth gaped open. "They can't do that, can they? Human's buy that, too."

"I'm not worried about humans right now. Steroids don't sit well with shifters. They also absorb it faster. Take the normal human side effects and multiply it by ten."

"Oh god."

"You need to understand that each clan has a hierarchy. Consider how the supplement will affect a clan when given to the alpha."

"Is that what's happening to him?"

"You mean Tobias?" I asked.

"Yeah. How do you know him?"

"I grew up with him. I left the clan nine years ago."

Her eyes grew wide. "You're a shifter," she whispered.

"Yes. But that's just between you and me. Understood?"

She nodded. "Do you think Tobias will be okay?"

I narrowed my eyes and studied her. She looked pale behind her curly red hair.

"He should be if we can convince him to stop taking the supplement. Why are you so worried about Tobias and not anyone from the Granite Bear Pack?"

Her cheeks turned bright red. "I'm worried about them, too. They just aren't taking as much as Tobias."

I shook my head with a sigh. I couldn't imagine what a woman like Cindy saw in Tobias. "Don't worry about anything now. I'm going to try to fix this. I'll talk to Arthur and Mac after I come back. Hopefully, I'll have a better idea of the situation."

"Okay," she squeaked. "Do you want my help?"

I shook my head. "No. Thanks, though."

Chapter 7

Rachel

I found the café on a corner near downtown. It looked like an old apartment building where they refurbished the downstairs into storefronts. Balconies hung over the doors with signs hanging underneath. The first thing I noticed when I walked in were the trees. The trunks disappeared into holes in the floor above. I peeked into the pots. The tree passed through the floor and, I assumed, into the ground below.

I sat at the empty bar. A short, curvy woman came over. "What will it be? Coffee or spirits?" she asked with a soft voice.

I sighed. "As much as I want spirits, I'll settle for coffee. Do you have anything to eat here?" The clock on the wall read 1:30 p.m., and I'd missed lunch.

"We have a limited food menu. Today we have chicken salad, roast beef sandwiches, and tomato bisque."

"I'll have the chicken salad." I smiled at the lady.

"Thanks. My name is Zola, if you have any questions."

I rested my head on the bar. Oli would be home in a few hours, and we could talk. I didn't particularly want to talk anymore, though. We'd been close for years. His parents and my parents were always close friends. While we were only three years apart, our older siblings didn't want us around, so Oli and I stuck together as kids. And I'd been in love with him since I was fourteen.

He moved away two years later when his brother took over the clan. Oliver refused to fight and never came home. When Tobias told him to fight or leave, I knew what Oli would choose. That night, I snuck into his room and begged him to stay. I watched him pack, tears running down my face. He kissed my forehead and left.

"I'll see you again. Don't worry," he said before he left.

I hadn't seen him since then until today.

A tall lady walked over and handed me my coffee. She stopped and stared at me as I took a sip. I sniffed the air. Shifter. Of course, Oliver would find a shifter bar.

"The name makes sense now. I take it you're the owner?" I sipped the coffee again. "This is good."

"My wife and I own the place." She leaned forward on the bar. "You know Oliver?"

I scrunched my nose. Of course, I smelled like him. I rolled in his bed for twenty minutes. "Yeah."

"We don't get many bears around here."

Zola walked over and placed the chicken salad in front of me, then pulled down the taller lady, kissed her on the cheek, and walked off.

"You have got to be the tallest squirrel I've ever seen."

She laughed. The sound reverberated around the bar. The joy in the sound brought a small smile to my face. "You're the shortest bear."

"I'm only short for a shifter." I tried to pout, but it quickly became a smile. "I'm Rachel."

"Well, Rachel, I'm Salma. What brings you to town? Besides Oliver?"

"At this moment, I wish I had something to bring me here besides him." I picked at the food on my plate.

"So, you really came here to bring him back?"

My fork stopped mid-stab. I slowly looked up at her through my lashes. "Yeah. I take it he told you about our clan's current situation. I know he won't stay, and I won't ask him to, but he might be the only one that can help."

She nodded, dropped her elbows onto the bar, and propped her head into her hands. "What makes you think he won't stay once he goes back?"

"Just a feeling."

"You sound sad."

I shook my head and took a bite. "I thought he'd look miserable. He left nine years ago, and for some reason, I thought he'd be pining to come back. He's not miserable here. He's not miserable without me."

"Did you know you were mates when he left?"

"What?" my jaw hit the floor. "But how…"

"Just a hunch." She smirked. "I take it you just found out? I don't think you need to worry about where he's going to end up. I think you need to worry about where you'll both end up. As long as it's the same place, right?"

"It's not that easy."

"It never is. I didn't want to move here, but I met Zola. And she took care of her sick mom, so she couldn't meet me halfway. It was scary but worth it. Being with your mate always is."

"You give Oli this kind of advice all the time, don't you? I can just see him sitting here talking to you."

She laughed. "It's true."

"How can y'all live here without a pack?"

"Being a rogue shifter can be difficult. We build our own disenfranchised pack out here. It's not so bad."

"It still would have been nice for him to look miserable without me."

"Oh honey, he was." She patted my arm. "Who do you think he talks about the most?"

"You're just saying that."

"Rachel West. Right?"

My eyes flew open and my heart beat faster.

"You work at a diner, have two brothers, and want to become a pastry chef."

I sat back in the bar chair. My arms felt limp.

"You're the only one he talks about besides his brother. It's nice to put a face to the name."

I could only smile before I turned my attention back to my lunch. She patted my head and walked away. A warmth filled my heart, and a smile played on my lips.

Chapter 8

Oliver

The entire day ended with more questions than answers. I sifted through files instead of visiting the doctors on my list. The information on Brawn-tality disturbed me. According to the public files, the supplement's official contents included typical ingredients that encouraged muscle growth, and anti-inflammatory agents considered supplements. When I dug deeper, I discovered the pill had just enough anabolic steroids to go undetected. This gave humans just a slight boost as long as they followed the directions on the bottle.

Shifters, however, were extremely sensitive to anabolic steroids. Side effects from even a small dose included irritability, increased anger, depression, and insomnia, all times ten. Even if taken appropriately, Tobias shouldn't have such a strong reaction to the drug. How much did he take at a time? I sighed. Of course, he'd take extra if he thought it prevented 'Shifter's Disease'.

I informed Mac I'd be taking Monday and Tuesday off for vacation, then walked out of the office with a memory stick full of files in my pocket. The time to return to Flint River Clan had arrived.

I saw the lights on inside as soon as I drove up to my house. I parked next to an old single-cabin truck in my driveway. A decal in the back window read 'Bake the World a Better Place'. The old truck belonged to her father once. I practically ran to the front door, knowing Rachel was inside my house.

I walked into the door, and the smell of biscuits hit me. A crazy grin popped up on my face. It'd been nine years since I had biscuits made by anyone from home and Rachel's family made the best ones.

Our parents were close, so dinners at each other's houses happened often. I remember the first time Rachel made biscuits. They looked lumpy, misshapen, and almost burnt, but she pulled them out of the oven and handed the first one to me. Her expectant look worried me. I didn't want to lie if they tasted terrible. I bit down into the crispy outside, into the soft, delicious bread inside. Delicious.

Now, she baked biscuits just for me. Rachel's

distinct scent snuck through under the smell of biscuits. My cock twitched. I suddenly didn't want food.

She stood in front of the stove, stirring something in a pot. I peeked down at the mashed potatoes and then straight into her eyes, now turned on me. "You cooked for me."

"Yeah. I couldn't just sit around and do nothing." She reached up her hand and cupped my cheek. "Hungry?"

"Yes."

I took her hand off the spoon and pushed her against the counter. I caressed her face with my hand and leaned in, lightly kissing her lips. Her hands gripped my shirt at the waist as my fingers sunk into her short, soft hair.

I licked her lips, and she granted me entrance. We tasted each other, tongues clashing. I hummed happily and kissed down her neck. Her moans sounded like music. She pulled my shirt up and ran her warm hands over my back.

My hands slid down her body and landed on her plump bottom. She arched into me and rubbed her body against mine. I knew she could feel my hard dick, especially when I pulled her closer.

"Do you know how long I've wanted to do this?" I whispered into her ear. My first sex dream starred her, but I could tell her that later.

"I didn't know you fantasized about fucking me in your kitchen." Her leg wrapped around my waist.

"I've fantasized about fucking you everywhere."

She clung tighter to me as if her leg had given out from under her. "Tell me more."

I growled and spun her around, bending her over the kitchen table. I tugged at her pants, desperate to pull them off.

BEEEEEEP. BEEP. BEEP. BEEEEEEP.

We both paused and looked at the oven.

"Biscuits." She sat up and pushed past me. She took the bread out of the oven and turned it off. "Do you want to eat?"

I walked over and leaned over her to turn off all the stove burners. Our eyes met. "Dinner can wait."

Her mouth curved into a smirk. I felt her hands tug on my belt as she led me away from the stove. "Where would you like your first fantasy to take place?"

I took a sharp breath in. She let me push her toward the table. In one quick movement, I slid her jeans and underwear down and lowered myself to my knees. I could smell her sweetness. I looked up at her. She stared down at me with big eyes and raised brows.

"The place I want to start is right here." I placed my hands on her wide hips and buried my face between her legs, giving her core a lick.

She yelped and leaned on the table. I grabbed a leg and swung it over my shoulder, sinking my face deeper between her thighs. She tasted just like she smelled, peaches and vanilla. I wanted her to cum all over my face.

My tongue teased her clit, spurred on by the sounds she made. I wanted her scent to be ingrained forever here in my kitchen, on the table. When I looked around my home, I wanted it to be filled with memories of Rachel, naked and wanting.

The more I licked and sucked, the less time I wanted to wait before I sunk my cock into her delicious pussy. I slowed down my pace until her hand gripped my hair and pushed me deeper in, and rubbed herself on my face.

I chuckled. "Yes, ma'am."

With renewed vigor, I clutched her ass and continued to devour her. Her body wiggled, her moans grew louder, and her legs squeezed my head. With one last lick, she reached her peak and crashed around me. Her body jolted, scooting the table back and forth under her. I kept her steady while lapping her up.

Her heavy pants filled me with pride. She pulled my face away from her center and looked down at me. Her blue eyes dilated and her cheeks were rosy. I pulled off my shirt and wiped my face. No words were spoken as I stood up and carried her to my bed.

She pulled me down with her on top of the comforter. Our mouths met, desperate for more. We pulled off our remaining clothes and flung them around the room. My first look at her fully naked took my breath away. I didn't deserve her, but I'd never give her back. I'd follow her anywhere.

~

Rachel

After the orgasm in the kitchen, I felt out of breath. But now, with him straddling my hips, his dark eyes worshiped the sight of me. I reached up and traced my fingers down his sculpted chest. He'd never been as big as the other shifters, but he was just as strong.

His hard muscles twitched under my touch. I stopped right at the tip of his long, thick dick. Pre-cum dripped down the side. He moaned when I wrapped my fingers the best I could around it, my fingertips not touching, and pumped up and down.

"Who knew you were hiding such a sexy body under that suit?" I grabbed his arm and pulled him down into a kiss.

He rubbed his bearded face all over my neck, kissing and licking it until he decided to move to my breast. That beard felt amazing between my legs, too. His tongue circled my sensitive nipple, sending tingles straight to my clit. I squirmed beneath him, my pussy already aching for him.

He moved to my other nipple, nipping and tugging at the hardened bud. I moaned and bucked under him. My hand pumped his dick faster. He stopped my hand and used his knee to open up my legs.

"I can't wait any longer." He whispered.

"Me either."

He pulled a condom out of the drawer of his nightstand and slid it on. He settled between my inviting thighs. The tip of his member slowly pressed into my core. I stretched around him, taking more than I thought possible. When he stopped moving, I couldn't help but gyrate my hips. His moan sent shivers down my body.

My legs wrapped around his waist, pulling him in deeper. "Don't stop now."

He growled in my ear and nipped at my neck. "You feel so good. I'm going to move now."

"Yes."

The thrusts started slowly until I couldn't stand it anymore and tried to speed things along. He bit down on my shoulder for a second. "Patience, I want to savor you."

"I'm out of patience," I panted.

"Is that so?" He looked down at me with an eyebrow raised.

I swallowed hard and nodded.

"May I mark you?"

"Yes." The breathless response that escaped surprised me.

He grinned, full canines showing. Receiving a claiming mark would seal our bond. The permanent scar served as a signal to other shifters and as a symbol of our connection. Before I could think, he'd pulled out and flipped me over onto my hands and knees. He spread my legs apart again and slipped back inside. My back arched at the sensation.

His hand wrapped lightly around my neck, and he pumped in and out of me. I didn't recognize the noises I made. My eyes rolled back in my head, and the bear inside panted. The only thing keeping me from dropping my shoulder onto the mattress was the light hold he had on my neck.

He pumped hard. My tits swung with the motion, and each thrust pushed me further to my breaking point. His body covered my back, the hand around my neck dropped to the bed, and his other reached around and rubbed my clit.

My nipples brushed against the sheets, and he pinched my nub. I could feel my body edge toward ecstasy when he bit down on the nape of my neck, sending me over completely. He yelled my name as he toppled over with me, holding me tight as we both sailed through the climax.

We collapsed on the bed together. He dropped to the side of me and pulled my back to him, licking and kissing the mark he gave me.

"I want to mark you again," he said.

I rolled over to face him. Dark eyes met mine. "As long as I can mark you first."

He pulled me close and hid his face in my neck. "Do you know how long I've loved you?"

My heart pounded at his words. "No," I whispered.

"It was after I left. Maybe a year after. One day you didn't answer my call. At the time, I couldn't stop the tears from falling. You're the only person, the only thing I miss from the clan."

"Why didn't you come to visit?" My hand rubbed circles on his back.

"Fear." He pulled back and looked me in the eye. "Fear that you weren't my mate. I didn't think I'd be able to come back from that."

I couldn't stop the huff of laughter that escaped me. I kissed him.

"Don't laugh at me." His fingers tickled my sides, then he stopped. "Are you crying?"

I rested my forehead on his. "That's the same reason I never came to visit you. I've been in love with you since I was fourteen. I longed and feared the day I turned eighteen. But then you left, and I didn't want to know the truth."

"We're a couple of idiots." He sunk his head into my neck again. "Did you lay in my bed today? Before I came home?"

"I don't see how that's any of your business."

"You don't?" He pounced on me, straddling me on all fours. "What am I going to do with you?"

"What do you want to do with me?"

"It might be faster to tell you what I don't want to do with you." He kissed me with the same desperation. "I don't think I'll ever have enough of you."

"Good." I rolled us over, so I sat on top.

My mouth met his again in a fever of kisses, each more desperate than the last. Being so close to him, knowing how he felt before we even knew our connection, gave me goosebumps. His kiss sent twinges of electricity throughout my body. I wanted more of him now. I felt his cock grow under me. I rubbed my wetness over his hardening length.

"Are you sure?" he asked.

"Yes. As long as you are."

He leaned forward and took my nipple into his mouth. The sensation caused my pussy to pulse. I leaned over to grab another condom when he wrapped his tongue around my other nipple. I moaned before I could stop myself. His powerful hands kneaded my ass as he tugged on my nipple with his teeth.

He continued to flick my hard buds while I put a new condom on him. His touch had me ready for another round. I grabbed his wrists and pushed them over his head. His lips melted into mine. I gently lowered onto his stiff dick beneath me. We moaned in unison as I took him all in. I dropped my face into his neck and started to pump my hips up and down.

Oli nipped at my ears and kissed my shoulder. I kept his hands trapped above his head and licked his neck from his shoulder all the way to his earlobe.

"You feel amazing," I said, moving my hips faster.

He gasped and moaned under me. I liked how he responded, how I responded when we were here together. My teeth grazed his neck. The hips under me bucked to meet my thrust. My vagina tightened. His eyes rolled back, and I bit down on his chest. I felt him tense and shatter, my own orgasm not far behind. I slowed my hips, savoring how he jerked and moaned with each movement.

Those dark eyes shone at me. "You're absolutely beautiful."

I stretched out on top of him, exhausted and content. "We should go eat," I mumbled, eyes closed.

"Five more minutes, then we'll go." He kissed my head and wrapped his arms around me. "How do you feel about spanking?"

"Hum, I'd love to spank that ass of yours." I giggled.

"That wasn't what I was thinking, but I won't say no."

No amount of handholding could compare to laying wrapped in his arms.

"Do you know how happy it made me to know you've fantasized about me?" I covered my face to hide my blush.

"Why's that? Have you fantasized about me as well?" He rubbed my back.

"Yes. I've been in love with you since I was fourteen." I turned my face back to watch his expression.

A smile slowly spread across his face. "Yeah?"

"Yeah." I smiled back. "We had just gotten off the bus from school and were walking down the road toward the clan's territory. I was fourteen, and you were seventeen. You usually got a ride from someone else in the clan, but I'd asked you to ride the bus with me that day, because...well I don't remember why now. We were talking about nothing and you suddenly presented me with a sucker."

His eyes sparkled as I talked.

I took a deep breath. "You said, 'I stopped by the gas station this morning on the way to school and I saw this sucker. You used to love this flavor when you were a kid. So, I bought it for you.' You smiled like you always did at me. I took the sucker from your hand and in that moment, I knew I loved you. I'd never been more scared and excited in my life. In the end, I never said anything."

His hand sunk into my hair and he looked straight at me. "I love you so much."

He kissed me like I'd just come home from war. He poured himself into that kiss, sucking on my tongue, then lips. I nipped at him when he pulled away. He rolled us over so he hovered over me. Kisses covered my neck and chest.

"What about dinner?" I asked.

He looked up at me with a single eyebrow raised. "I'm about to have seconds."

Chapter 9

Oliver

The next morning, I dragged myself out of bed, packed a bag, and printed up a stack of documents from the memory stick I loaded yesterday. This took more time than planned because of the distraction lazing across my bed, gazing at me with her beautiful blue eyes. We took several breaks to satisfy the seemingly unquenchable need between us.

I expected Rachel to ask how long I'd stay at the Flint River Clan or to ask me to stay permanently. The desire to ask her to move here stayed at the back of my mind. Both of us avoided the discussion, prolonging it as long as possible.

We stood in front of our cars after I locked up my house.

"We'll take my truck," she said right before I opened my mouth to suggest taking mine.

Did she read my mind? If we took different vehicles, we would separate that much more quickly. This way, we had two long car rides together. She grabbed my bag and threw it into the bed of the truck. I watched her climb in the cab. The truck came to life, and she rolled down the passenger side window. "You comin'?"

What if our thoughts were not the same? My mind went in circles. If I left with her, would I be able to leave? Did she plan on coming back with me? Did she plan to drive me back or have someone else drive me?

Her loud sigh cut through my thoughts. "Get in. I'll give you a ride back."

"I don't want to take up your time."

"I want to spend as much time with you as I can. I need to make up for the last nine years." Her smile melted away my insecurities, and I climbed into the truck.

She reversed out of the driveway, then drove out of my small subdivision. "First things first. You need to hear all the songs I had to listen to while you were gone."

"What are you talking about?" I stared at her while she hit a button on her phone. Apparently, she'd installed a Bluetooth car adapter in the decades old truck as the music started to play over the speakers.

My jaw dropped as "Cotton Eye Joe" blasted into the cabin. "What is wrong with you?"

She laughed. "It's what you deserve for being gone for nine years."

"You know you have to listen to it as well."

Her hand squeezed my thigh. "Worth it."

Once south of I-285 on the backroads, I could feel my wolf pacing back and forth inside me. He wasn't looking forward to going back, either. Rachel reached over and put her hand on my leg to stop it from shaking.

"Sorry." I gave her a small smile. "I guess I'm a little nervous."

She grabbed my hand and squeezed it. "I know. You don't need to apologize."

I concentrated on the warmth of her hand.

"Do you still like working at the diner?"

Her smile didn't reach her eyes. "I do. Uncle Eddie lets me make the desserts and the bread. Then I have to help with the prep and fill in for any missing cooks."

"You made the best peach cobbler. Do you still make it?"

"I do, but only in the summer. It's no longer peach season."

"I wish it were always peach season. You smell like peaches, you know." I sniffed the air and winked at her.

"Well, I got some peach cobbler for you." She

laughed at her own joke.

"That's a strange sexual innuendo. It may need some work."

"It doesn't need work if you know what I'm talking about." She rubbed her thumb against my hand. "What about you? You still like your job? Selling pharmaceuticals?"

"I did until I found out the company is blatantly ignoring the side effects of shifters. It's probably much worse than that. I'll need to look for a new job soon. I can't sell Brawn-tality to a pack. The data they have on humans is probably false as well. It's so fucked up."

"What kind of job will you look for?"

I looked out the window and watched the fields pass us by. "Maybe I'll go into Real Estate. My favorite part of the job is the people. And I really enjoy looking at housing sites."

"Guilty pleasure?"

"That's right. I don't think taking a realtor class costs too much. I can get a temporary job at a different pharmaceutical company while I change careers. Dunnam Graham offered me a sales job a few weeks ago. It might still be on the table."

"Lucky."

"Nah, we build our own luck. Things don't drop in our lap if we do nothing. I build connections, and that's how the offer came about. It wouldn't happen if I didn't put myself out there."

"You know, there's a pastry school just south of Alpharetta. It's part of the Art Institute of Atlanta. I haven't told anyone, but I applied a few months ago."

She stared out the windshield as she spoke; my attention was solely on her.

"I got the acceptance letter last week. Uncle Eddie saw the pamphlet with my stuff and told me to apply. I'm glad I have his support. It's scary to think about leaving. I don't know how you did it."

"I didn't think I had a choice back then. Instead of looking for another pack, I disconnected myself from the shifter world. I basically jumped into the unknown, and I was terrified. But I had your voice to look forward to each week."

"You're all flattery."

"It's true," I said. Her cheeks flushed for a moment. "I'll catch you. If you decide to jump."

She glanced my way for just a second. A smile spread across her lips. "I'll keep that in mind."

I kissed the back of her hand I still held. "I want you to be happy. No matter what."

"And what would make you happy?"

"Um…" I sighed. "You."

My cheeks burned with the confession. I felt silly and hid my face with her hand.

"I know that. But what else?" she laughed.

I laughed, too. "A pool in my backyard, a peach tree that produces peaches year-round, and for Tobias to not punch me in the face when he sees me."

"I think only one of those is doable. I thought

you'd say a maid."

"I have a cleaning service. They come in once every two weeks."

"Fancy, schmancy man. You have a lawn service, too?"

"I do. But only for the grass. I don't know if you noticed, but I have a few flower beds around the house. I like to garden."

"How did gardening suddenly seem so sexy to me?"

"Are you picturing me naked, pulling weeds?"

"I wasn't, but I am now. Just you in a large hat and gloves."

I scooted closer to her. "Sounds like a great idea to me. Want to join me in this naked garden fantasy?"

"Only if I can put a tiny hat on your penis."

"Deal. I'll make sure you have hats for your nipples, like tassels, only hat shaped."

Laughter echoed in the truck. Her cheeks looked rosy, and her eyes sparkled. Making my mate laugh became a new daily goal. Nothing sounded sweeter than her happiness.

By the time she drove onto clan land, we'd put hats on most of our body parts in the fantasy. The mood turned sour the deeper we got into the territory.

"How long do you think it will take for him to realize I'm here?" I watched the familiar trees as we passed.

"A day, I hope."

"I can only hope. I'm not exactly prepared to see him after all this time."

She turned down the road that takes you around the north perimeter of the clan's land. On the south side of the territory stood the Old Flint Farm where most of the clan worked, including Tobias, Rachel's parents, and brothers.

Acres of peaches grew on the south end. Blackberry patches grew north of the peaches and the vegetable fields sat to the east of the blackberries. They turned half the peaches and blackberries into jellies, jams, and preserves. The diner got first pick of the vegetables. They sold the rest to other restaurants, at the clan's roadside stand, and local fairs. Most of the money came from the peaches, blackberries, and the jams. The farm shipped them all around the country.

Tobias and I planned to run it together one day. He enjoyed tending to the blackberries, and I favored the peach orchard. Before our father died, Tobias planned to grow blueberries. I wanted to include spicy peppers to add variety to our jellies and jams. I didn't realize it then, but my idea of pepper jelly came from Rachel. She loved to spread it on crackers with cream cheese.

I always assumed that he would become Alpha and I the second-in-command. We planned to grow the farm, expand the online business, and start having big events for the holidays, like blackberry picking, a pumpkin patch, or even a festival. In the end, I wasn't around to see the implementation of any of our ideas. I only heard about it through Rachel.

"My home is about as far away from the clan center as you can get and still be in the territory," Rachel said, bringing me out of my thoughts.

"The old James' house?"

Peter James built a house far away from the rest of the clan fifty years ago when his wife suddenly died. He passed about a year before I left. He kept to himself but was a good man.

"Yeah. I always liked the house, and it's nice and quiet in the evenings. It's even better because I usually don't have to deal with Tobias now." She took a deep breath. "I hope he listens to you. We may need to confiscate his supply."

I gave a noncommittal sound. Tobias could be stubborn, and with the influence of steroids, he was probably much worse than normal. We passed the old oak that marked the halfway point to the old James' house. I suppose I could call it the West house now. I remember racing to that oak tree to climb it with Tobias. Carved initials and hearts covered the lower half of the tree. The clan had a superstition which said if you carved your initials on the tree with the one you wanted, they would become your mate. Of course, you had to do that before you turned 18. My mom told me it came true for her.

At seventeen, the prospect of finding my mate

terrified me. I couldn't fathom falling instantly in love with someone I didn't know or hated. I didn't share that fear with anyone, but somehow Tobias dragged it out of me. He laughed and told me to think of one person I thought I'd like to see every day and carve their initials in the tree with my own.

I could only think of Rachel at the time. Little 14-year-old Rachel, who I liked to tease and could carry on a sensible conversation. She would rather climb a tree than paint her nails and never shied away from what she liked.

One night a month before I turned 18, I climbed that tree almost to the top and carved our initials on a branch. To think I'd forgotten something like that until now. Rachel slowly drove down the gravel road. I reached over and brushed my hand along her cheek. She looked at me; her face lit up with a smile. When she turned back to the road, she slammed on the brakes.

My hand hit the dash, and I looked up to see Tobias standing in the middle of the road. He breathed heavily and flared his nostrils. I couldn't believe how much bigger he looked than when I left. Dark circles under his eyes told me he hadn't slept. Scratches covered his forearms. Mud caked the knees of his jeans, and part of his shirt was ripped, exposing his right side.

"Oliver." He barely made a sound, but I could hear him just fine. "Did you think I wouldn't smell you?"

He used the alpha voice used to help keep the pack in line. I felt Rachel shiver beside me, but it didn't have any effect on me. He wouldn't like that one bit.

"Why are you here?"

I rolled down the window and stuck my head out. "Just came for a visit. Don't worry. I'm not staying."

"Get out here and talk to me face to face." His voice gradually became louder.

I turned to Rachel and said, "Aren't we face-to-face now?"

She rolled her eyes at me, but I couldn't stop my laugh. I opened the truck door.

"Don't," Rachel whispered.

"It's fine." I closed the door behind me and walked over to my brother.

"You have ten minutes to get off of our property."

"I'm just here for a quick visit. Give me 24 hours."

"Why'd you drag her into this?"

I looked back. She white-knuckled the steering wheel. "There was no dragging involved."

"I won't give you the ashes."

I frowned. Did he mean our mom's ashes? "I don't need the ashes."

"I'm not feeding you." He scratched the side exposed by the ripped shirt.

"I'm heartbroken. Never thought you'd learn to cook."

"And there's nothing left in the box. You can't

have it."

"What are you talking about?" I couldn't follow his logic. How did he jump from ashes to food to an unknown box?

"You know what I'm talking about. You're here to challenge me, aren't you?"

"Why would I sneak around to do that? Are you really worried I would beat you in a fight?"

"Why are you always like this? You never give a straight answer." Tobias practically yelled.

"You never liked my straight answers."

"JUST TELL ME WHY YOU'RE HERE." His yell hurt my ears.

"I'm here to see Rachel."

"Why?" he said, his voice low and deep.

"Cause I love her and couldn't stay away any longer."

His eyes practically bulged out of his head, and I could see how red the whites of his eyes looked. "Don't take away any of my women."

My stomach dropped. Everything I had heard over the last few weeks was true. None of it is exaggerated. If anything, they downplayed his condition. The person before me couldn't be my brother, could he? Before I could stop myself, I said, "What's wrong with your eyes?"

He growled. His fist hit me before I realized he'd moved. I managed to move out of the way of his second punch. As long as I stayed between him and Rachel, I could deal with whatever he threw my way.

The hair on his body began to lengthen, and his voice deepened. "Nothing is wrong with me." He roared into the sky, his arms stretched out beside him.

If I didn't act now, he'd shift and I wouldn't stand a chance of making it out without major injuries. I stepped forward and punched him in the kidney, and followed up with an uppercut to the chin. Despite my small build, I packed a punch.

He backed up, holding his chin. "Stop. Kneel before me," he used his alpha voice to command me.

I stayed on the balls of my feet, ready to move at any moment. "That won't work on me."

"KNEEL, OLIVER." The power behind it vibrated in my chest. His face and neck turned red as he stared into my eyes.

I stared right back. Why wasn't he shifting? "I'm not part of your pack."

Sweat slid down the sides of his face. "You can't have her." His voice came out small, like a child's.

"She's my mate, Tobias."

He let go of his chin. It looked almost purple. Shifters healed fast, but I had a bad feeling about how his chin looked.

"Are you healing slower than normal?" I fought my urge to drop my defenses and inspect his wound.

"What kind of question is that?"

"Your chin doesn't look right."

"You just punched me there. Of course, it doesn't

look right." He spat on the ground. "You fuckin' bastard."

I looked back at Rachel and raised my eyebrows. Should I say something? I wondered if she was thinking the same thing. She nodded. I decided to trust my instinct.

Turning back to Tobias, I said, "I heard that some shifters were taking that supplement Brawn-tality, and it had some nasty side effects. You should check to see if anyone here is trying it. Heard it contained a low dose of steroids."

He narrowed his eyes and sneered. "You have twelve hours. Not a second more."

I noticed the hair on his arms starting to grow. I backed up to the truck and climbed in before he could shift. Rachel didn't say a word, and we drove past him. Tobias and I didn't take our eyes off each other until Rachel drove me out of sight.

Tobias and I were always close as kids. It broke my heart when he told me to leave or fight. How did we let the divide between us get so deep? Now it seemed unbridgeable.

~

Rachel

"Fuck. What were you thinking?" I parked in front of my house.

It resembled an old log cabin on the outside but,

thankfully, didn't have wood paneling on the inside. I loved the long, covered front porch with the porch swing. The outside flower beds didn't look as nice at Oli's. I kept the mix of boxwood and holly that Old Man James planted. With too many trees around my place, it didn't get too much sunlight. I figured the more colorful plants wouldn't grow. The only thing I really needed were the herbs I grew in the kitchen.

The house had two bedrooms, one of which I filled with books and my crochet projects. I used the other as my own nightly hibernation station. I could get the room pitch black, run the fan at full blast, and burrow into my pile of blankets.

"Which part?"

"You didn't have to get out of the truck."

"I didn't want him to get you involved." He climbed out of the truck and grabbed his bag from the back.

I followed him up the front steps to my door. "You are playing a dangerous game with him. You didn't have to hit him back."

He sighed. "He didn't have to hit me first. He's worse than anyone said."

We walked into the house. I sat with Oliver on the couch. I only sat in the living room when crocheting or when people visited. Unlike my sports obsessed brothers, my TV remained small and sat on a stand in the corner.

I really bought this house for the kitchen. I don't

know why Peter James added such a large kitchen, but I never complained. The counter space fit my pastry making needs perfectly. Even after living here for three years, I still had room in the cabinets to fill.

"He's not making much sense anymore," I said. "He's worse than he was two days ago. Seemed to keep focus better after you hit him."

"That's just what he needs. Percussive maintenance."

I shook my head, then pulled him toward me. Oliver's left eye looked a little swollen from the hit he took. I lightly touched it, and he flinched.

"It doesn't look too bad."

He grinned at me. "Does it make me look dangerous?"

I laughed. "No. Not one bit."

I stood, only for him to drag me into his lap and cover me in kisses. Giggles erupted from me as I wiggled to get out of his grasp. I started to fall off his lap, but his hands grabbed my waist and pulled me back up. I grinned at him, then dissolved into another round of giggles when he continued to tickle me.

"Ew. Gross. Hands off my sister."

We stopped and looked up at my brother standing three feet in front of us. We didn't even hear the door open.

"Hey, Coby," I said, pausing with one leg sticking straight out.

Coby was the same age as Tobias and his second in command. He also towered over everyone in the pack. We shared the same blue eyes and brown hair, though he appeared lanky because of his height. In reality, he had a decent gut, which his mate liked to rub for luck.

Coby and his mate, Abby, allowed me to crash on their couch several nights a week since Tobias started acting strange. Our oldest brother, Daven, let me stay the other nights, but Coby preferred me to stay with him. Despite being the middle child, he was overprotective of me. He only trusted a handful of people to keep me safe.

Daven and I had a thirteen-year age difference between us. When I turned five, he'd already moved out of the house. When I turned ten, he taught me to fight. He trusted me to take care of myself. It took Coby longer to realize I didn't need his constant protection.

"I see you convinced Oliver to come back. How've you been, man?"

"Good." Oliver didn't move a muscle. "You?"

"Good." He nodded his head, looking at the two of us. "Whatcha doin' to my sister?"

Oli turned his eyes to me and then back to my older brother. "Tickling her?"

"You smell like each other, and it's gross. At least get off his lap while I'm here."

I pushed off of Oli. My cheeks burned. Of course, my idiot brother would walk into my place without knocking.

"So, Oliver, do you think you can help?" He sat on one of the chairs across from the couch. He rubbed his palms on his knees, a nervous habit from when he was younger.

"I hope so. I think I know the cause of his behavior."

"Which is?"

"Have you seen him taking a supplement called Brawn-tality?"

"Son of a bitch." He stood up and walked out of the room. Two minutes later, he returned with a beer from my fridge. "He's been popping them for the last month. Some shifter chick convinced him to try them. He's enamored with her. She doesn't smell right to me."

"That's cause she's not a shifter." Oli looked at the ceiling. "There is apparently a mixture that can change your scent when ingested. It makes humans smell like a nondescript shifter."

Coby drank half the beer in one go. "What's with the pills then? I've read the bottle. Shouldn't cause us any problems."

"It has a low dose of steroid in it that they haven't listed."

"Damn. How did you find this out?"

Oli's head dropped in his hand.

"He works for the pharmaceutical company. And with that woman." I scratched Oli's head.

Coby downed the rest of the bottle. "I might still be too sober for this."

"Stop. I can't send you home drunk. Abby will kill you." I took the bottle from him. "No more for you."

"Geez. Do you have any good news for me?"

"He should go back to normal if he stops taking the medicine. We just need to convince him to stop."

"Not sure if that's good news. Just sounds like we need more help."

"Who do you think will help? I'm thinking Haze and Gray." I held up two fingers.

"Daven will help, and probably Fern and Pine," Coby added.

"What about the elders?" Oli asked.

"I'm sure they will help. We just need a plan." I tapped my toes and leaned on Oli. I felt him kiss the top of my head.

"Any other good news?" Coby widened his eyes and looked expectantly between Oli and me.

"Um...no," I said. Oli hid his head behind my back, shaking with laughter as soon as the words left my lips.

"You're the worst sister. It's not like I can't tell you're mates, but you could have the common decency to tell me instead of playing games." He frowned and crossed his arms over his broad chest.

"But your expressions are worth it every time. I should have taken a picture for Abby." I laughed.

"Don't give my mate more fuel against me. She teases me enough as it is." Coby ran his fingers through his hair. "And congratulations. You hurt my sister and you're dead. Now let's get everyone together so we can fix Tobias."

Chapter 10

Oliver

Everyone arrived at Rachel's within thirty minutes of calling. Much faster than I imagined. Tobias's new personality lost him support in the community.

Two hours passed and loud disagreements filled Rachel's home. Rachel and her brother, Cobalt, or Coby, as everyone called him, didn't see eye to eye on any of the plans. Someone drew a map of Tobias's house and the surrounding area. Haze, Gray, Rachel, and Coby stood around the kitchen table and argued. Haze and Gray were mates and worked as private detectives.

Pine and Fern sat at the table. Fern doodled little trees on the map as the three argued above them. Fern apparently came from a different pack. She joined as soon as she met her mate, Pine.

Daven, Rachel's oldest brother, leaned against the counter next to me watching the four argue. He shook my hand and congratulated me as soon as he walked in the door. Then he told me that if I hurt Rachel, he'd sell tickets for everyone to watch her kill me. The threat hit harder than Coby's.

Haze and Gray threw up their hands and walked away from the debate. Now the six of us watched Rachel and Coby continue their heated discussion. They forgot that I'd need to do the hard work, and they were the support. The only thing we all agreed on was that those helping would prevent others from interfering once I went in to talk to Tobias.

"We need to get all the supplements out of his house tonight." Rachel poked Coby's chest with her finger.

He swatted her hand away. "That's ridiculous. He'll know something is up first thing in the morning. And I've told you, he's not sleeping like he should. He'll know as soon as you enter the house."

"What was your plan again? Wait for Tobias to come to his senses and let him hand over his supply?"

I leaned over to Daven. "When should we step in?"

"Give it five more minutes." He smirked.

I heard him snicker several times over the last 20 minutes. "You're enjoying this, aren't you?"

"Of course." His eyes laughed. "So, you think you'll come back here, or do you think she'll leave

"I don't know."

She cupped my face with her hands. "It felt similar to an alpha voice, but different. I've only felt cold when it's been used on me, but you, your voice, warmed me. It felt weird."

"I don't know what to tell you. It isn't something I've ever done before. At least, I don't think I have."

She kissed me and rubbed her face on mine. "I'm scared," she whispered.

"Tomorrow's going to be hard. We should get some sleep." I kissed down her neck onto her shoulder.

She stood up and pulled me with her. "Sleep, you say?"

I couldn't resist her soft smile. I floated behind her into her bedroom. The walls were dark purple, with canvas paintings hanging on the wall. Blankets were piled high on her bed. A single light shone from her bedside table.

She pulled me close and kissed me. We were almost the same height, making kissing her easy. My hands ran up and down her body, stopping to grab a handful of her perfect ass. She moaned in my mouth.

She pulled my shirt over my head and pushed me onto the bed. After a moment of her standing over me, looking me up and down, she crawled on top of me, kissing up my body. Each touch made my cock twitch and come to life, one kiss at a time. Warmth rushed through my body with each stroke of her hands. When she finally kissed me square on the mouth, I was ready to explode.

Our mouths licked and bit at each other, desperate for more to taste. I frantically pulled her shirt off of her. Her breast hung in front of me, leaving me to wonder how long she'd been walking around without a bra. She flinched when I palmed her breast and pinched her nipple. I wanted to suck on her perky tits. She slid down my body before I had a chance.

Her hands unbuttoned my jeans and pulled them and my underwear down around my ankles. A gasp escaped me as she wrapped both hands around my stiff member. Those pink lips of hers slipped over the head of my dick. She spread her mouth to the limit for me. I never imagined her tiny mouth could stretch over me as it did now. She licked the underside of my dick where the head met the shaft. I fought the urge to thrust myself deeper into her mouth.

Her hands began to move along my length as she sucked on the head. I couldn't take my eyes off her. I swear I grew bigger; her eyes peeked at me through her lashes. When she moaned as she sucked, I knew I couldn't hold back if she didn't stop.

"Babe," I panted. "Rachel. Stop."

She hummed, then popped off my dick. "Why?"

"I'm going to cum if you don't stop."

She licked all around the head. "That's the plan."

"I wanna be inside you when I cum."

Her eyes widened, and her pupils grew. "That can be arranged."

She stood up, and I kicked off my pants around my feet. She bent over to grab something out of the bedside drawer. I took my chance and shimmied her out of her pants, leaving her gloriously naked in front of me. She turned with a smile and a condom in her hand.

On my knees with her ass in my face, I took a nibble out of each cheek. I bent her over and licked her sweet pussy from behind. She was so wet already. I stood up and slid a finger inside her wetness. I pulled my finger out and pinched her clit. Her yelp spurred me on.

She turned around and cupped my balls. "Why don't we crawl into the bed?"

~

Rachel

I started to back up to drag him to the bed, but he pulled me close and turned me around, so my ass pressed against his hard cock. He reached around and rubbed my clit. I shivered on contact and arched into him.

"Come on. Walk with me," he whispered in my ear.

He led me to the nearest wall and bent me over, placing my hands on the wall in front of me. His fingers slid down my angled back. I wiggled my ass, but he grabbed my hips.

"Not yet, sweetheart."

His touch burned my skin. I squirmed with each light touch. Hands cupped my breast, pinching and flicking my nipples. Each flick sent a bolt of electricity straight to my clit. My head dropped in a groan of pleasure.

"Hurry," I huffed out.

"Patience." He leaned over me and kissed me where he had marked me the day before.

My knees grew weak when he kissed me there. Only his hands holding my breasts kept me from hitting the floor. His soft laughter gave me chills. I felt one of his hands move down my body and cup my mound.

"I love how soft you are here." He found my clit and rubbed.

"Are you disappointed I don't shave all the hair away?"

"I like you the way you are."

I gasped at the feeling of his fingers plunging into me.

"So cute. So wet. Are you wet for me?"

"Yes," I managed to say.

Slipping out of my center, he pushed me down a little more. He pulled the condom out of my hands and I heard the wrapper open, then one hand grasped my hip, and his hard cock pushed at my entrance. He entered with one smooth thrust. The action sent tingles from my clit to my nipples.

"Use the voice." I wanted to feel the power while

he filled me.

He paused, then ran his hands up my body. "I love how you feel and how you look bent over. How the nape of your neck is exposed, and I can see my mark." I gasped. His thick voice rolled over me. The force in his voice felt like a burst of fire inside me, taking my breath away.

He brushed the mark with his fingers, and my cunt pulsed around him.

"Oh. That's nice," he said in his normal voice.

He touched the mark again and started to move. My head leaned back, my mouth open, but no sound came out. Each thrust created goosebumps all over my skin. I craved his touch all over my flushed body. I turned my head, trying to see his face as he fucked me.

His arm wrapped around my waist, and the other grabbed my hair, twisting my head even more. He leaned forward and kissed me. He let my head go and grabbed onto my hips, pounding me harder. Short squeaks and pants left my mouth with each hit. My arms and legs felt weak as pleasure enveloped my body.

"Oh, Rachel," he gasped behind me.

I couldn't form words. The only thing I knew was how close I was to the edge, but I didn't want to stop. I felt his hands travel around me and touch my hard nub. He rubbed my clit, and I panted harder. Before I knew it, I shouted and shuddered in Oli's arms. He followed quickly after.

My arms and legs felt like jelly, though my arms still propped me against the wall. His body covered my back, his heart pounding so hard I could feel it.

"You're so wonderful." He kissed my shoulder and slid out of me.

He carried me a few feet to my bed while I protested before disposing of the condom. He crawled into the bed with me, pulling me close.

"Can we do that again?" He kissed the side of my head.

I snuggled into his warm body. "Please. I'd like that."

He laughed. His hands roamed my body as we lay there together.

"I like your bed," he said.

"Oh yeah? It's pretty good. I wanted to find the perfect bed for my bear and me."

"Is she that picky?"

"No. She settled for you so..."

He tickled me when I giggled. I turned in his arms and kissed him. "I love you. You know that, right?"

His dark eyes sparkled, and his smile grew. "I love you, too."

I kissed him again. "I know. You already told me."

"You are a brat," he said, tapping my nose.

"I'm your brat."

Oliver squeezed me to his chest. "My brat."

~

Oliver

A single beam of sunlight broke through the curtains in the room. I woke up dreading the day, but with an arm full of fur. I didn't remember Rachel having a shaggy pillow, but the object in front of me smelled like Rachel. It grunted when I hugged it. With the blankets pulled off, a black bear slept curled up beside me. She looked the same as when I left, with a tan snout and ears, while the rest of her fur remained pitch black. She put a paw over her eyes when the light hit her.

"Am I to expect to wake up next to a bear every morning?"

A single blue eye opened and looked at me. She scooted toward me and licked my chest. I hated that she looked so adorable. I knew saying no to Rachel would be hard, but I never imagined having the same problem with her bear.

"I guess this explains the king-size bed and why you insisted on sleeping naked."

The wolf inside whined and jumped. He wanted to meet his mate, too. I sighed, climbed out of bed to take off my underwear, and then shifted. It was second nature to shift now. Our first shift happens when we hit puberty as if that time isn't hard enough.

My wolf jumped on the bed and curled around the bear. Her black bear dwarfed my wolf, but he snuggled his nose against hers and gave it a lick. I could hear her laugh through our mind link. As mates, we'd be able to communicate while shifted. The best part was feeling her emotions. I lay beside her, warming each other with our bodies, and I could feel her love for me. This felt like a peace I didn't deserve, but I refused to squander it.

I felt her wiggle and bury her head. I felt her sadness. With a huff, she shifted back into human form.

She petted me and I laid my head on her lap.

"Do you remember the first time I saw your wolf? I was running around my backyard with a big stick, pretending to fight monsters, when you jumped over one of our bushes. I stopped what I was doing because I'd never seen a wolf so beautiful before. You walked up, licked my face, and stole my stick. I was so mad." She laughed.

I lifted my head and laughed as a wolf, my tongue rolled out of the side of my mouth.

She scratched my head. "We have to face the day."

I shifted as well. "Sad we have to leave the bed?"

"Yes." She kissed me and stumbled out onto the floor.

She puttered around the room, grabbing clothes from her drawers while I watched her from the bed. I'd never felt more delighted. My naked mate walked around the room without hiding her body from my roaming eyes.

She looked at me over her shoulder. "Want to shower together?"

I practically jumped out of bed and followed her into the bathroom.

Chapter 11

Oliver

The morning dew still sat on the blades of grass when we assembled at the clan elder Stone's house. He didn't look a day past 50, but I knew he was pushing 80. His salt and pepper-colored hair gave him a distinguished look, but he dressed like a lumberjack. I'm sure his style appealed to his mate. As the oldest and most outspoken of the elected elders, he appreciated my presence. Well, after he gave me an earful for being gone for nine years.

The Flint River Clan had four elders at all times. Each one voted in by the pack and approved by the alpha. They could step down at any time. Rachel told me last night that Stone, Ivy, Briar, and Patrick were the current elders.

The elders mostly offered the clan and the alpha advice on everyday life, governing the clan, and maintaining a peaceful and safe environment for all. Myrtle created an extra responsibility for the elders, a monthly potluck dinner for everyone. I don't know when she stepped down, but I'm sure she still helped organize the potlucks.

The worst part of the elder's job included the responsibility of taking down the alpha should he or she step out of line. It fell under the 'maintaining a peaceful and safe environment' duty. I never expected it to be considered. As much as I'd grown apart from Tobias, I still did not want him to die.

"I understand you wanted to give your brother space to rule unopposed, but you could have at least called him to work things out outside of the clan." Stone's gruff voice didn't carry like it once did.

"I didn't change my phone number for three years. He had time to call me."

Stone smacked me across the back of my head. "You back talking me, son?"

I rubbed the spot. "Damn. Okay. You have a point."

"Once you go in, the other elders and I will call around to make sure no one goes to bother you. I take it the others here will stay outside to do the same? He'll feel outnumbered and defensive if too many people go with you."

"That's the plan. Only Rachel and Coby are going

in with me."

"Don't you think that's too many?" Stone looked around the room.

"I'm going to go in first. He'll feel like it's two on two," Coby said.

"His paranoia won't see it that way. You'll need to be out of the room when they start the conversation."

"Then I'll search while they talk." Coby nodded.

"Thanks, Stone," I squeezed his shoulder.

"If you manage to bring him back down to earth, be sure to come and visit. Oh, and Ivy will be mighty pissed if you fail."

"What do you mean?"

"She's a crack shot, but she'd rather not demonstrate the skill on the living."

I nodded and left Stone's house with Rachel and the others in tow. The five not going into the house spread out to approach from different angles. Coby pushed ahead and gave us a thumbs-up when he passed.

We slowed to give Coby time before we showed up.

"How do you think this is going to go?" Rachel asked

"It's going to be a shit show."

"You don't think he'll give up the pill easily?"

"No. He's stubborn. If he listens to the recording, we'll be doing good. I figure I can leave the paperwork and hope he at least reads it."

"What are you most worried about?"

"Us." I didn't even stop to think. Questions about where we would end up simmered under the surface. "I'll stay if you want me to stay."

She squeezed my hand. "You're such an idiot." She grinned up at me.

"What?" I asked.

"We're here."

She pulled me up the steps to the house I grew up in. It looked exactly the same, except for a fresh coat of red paint on the front door. The two-story brick home housed the alphas and their families for the last four generations.

The rocking chairs my mom used to sit on while she played the guitar and watched us play in the yard were still sitting on the porch. Someone recently refinished them. The porch had new stain, and the paint on the railings looked fresh. Obviously, Tobias took care of the house. I hated the situation he found himself in.

I opened the door without knocking. Tobias stood in the living room in shorts and a shirt talking to someone in the kitchen. He turned to look at us.

"What are you doing here?" The flatness in his voice surprised me.

"I wanted to talk to you before I left."

"I don't think that's necessary," he said, narrowing his eyes.

"Your chin still looks bad. It should be healed by

now."

He touched his swollen chin. It looked worse than the day before. My eye healed overnight.

"It's fine."

"Look. I work for Landry & Caddel. It's a pharmaceutical company."

"Congratulations." Tobias rolled his eyes.

Coby poked his head out of the kitchen, pointed to the back of the house, and then walked away. He'd hopefully clear the place of the pills before the conversation turned nasty.

"They make Brawn-tality. They pulled me into a meeting two days ago with a new job to convince shifter communities to take the supplement."

"What does that have to do with me?" He puffed out his chest.

"You're taking it. The pills contain steroids, and you know how dangerous that is to shifters."

"You're lying. She'd never suggest something like that to me." His eyes shot daggers my way.

I sighed. "She didn't know. I had to dig deep into the files at the company to find it."

"And what? You think you know her?" He took a few steps towards me.

Rachel grabbed my arm and said, "Easy."

"I do know Cindy. We work together."

"I don't believe you. This is just a trick to take over the clan."

"I've never wanted the clan." I pulled out my phone and hit play.

The hum of a recording started, and Cindy's voice floated from my phone:

Cindy: "Yes. Shifters are real. I have contacted two organizations. One refers to themselves as a pack, the other as a clan. Each has a variety of shifters."

Mac: "They can really shift into different animals? Like one person can be whatever animal they want?"

Dr. Thorne: "No. A shifter is born able to shift into one animal and not of their choosing. It would be the same as the animal their parents shift into."

Me: "And why will they want to use Brawn-tality?"

Cindy: "They are strong, but this could make them stronger and heal faster. It's perfect for a sick shifter or as a preventative measure against 'Shifter's Disease'."

Me: "Shifter's Disease…"

Cindy: "No one knows exactly what it is, only that when a shifter gets it, they die within days."

Mac: "And our product can really prevent it?"

Arthur: "We don't know that for sure. It might. We don't have the funding to test it, but it can't hurt."

Tobias tried to snatch my phone from my hand. I pulled it back, stopping the play back.

"No. She wouldn't." His face, ears, and neck turned red.

"She was doing her job, and they didn't tell her the side effects."

"How could she do this to another shifter?"

"She's not a shifter. She took a medicine that changed the way she smells."

"YOU'RE A LIAR."

He charged me, hitting me in the same spot as yesterday. When will I learn to dodge the first hit? I stumbled but didn't fall. He stayed on me and tried to punch me back. His fist hit the wall, and my elbow connected with his side.

"You little bitch," he said under his breath.

"Why are you fighting me? I just want to help." I motioned to Rachel. "Just look at the paperwork I found."

She waved the papers I printed from the memory stick I took from work.

"You don't want to help. You want to take over."

He barreled into me with his shoulder. I hit the ground hard enough to knock the wind out of me. He landed on top of me and then grabbed my arms. His eyes were bloodshot. Instead of his normal dark eyes, one looked golden, like his wolf wanted out.

He picked me up and threw me against the front door. I stumbled to pull myself up while gasping for breath.

"Tobias," I gasped. "I don't want to take over. You're a great alpha. I always knew you would be."

"But you're back. And you'll stay."

He ran toward me again. I dodged and tripped

him. He landed face down on the floor. Blood ran from his nose when he looked up.

"You'll stay because you found your mate." Tobias wiped his nose with his arm, smearing the blood across his face.

"We won't stay. Just stop taking those pills," Rachel said.

I looked over my shoulder. She pinched her lips together, and her eyebrows almost touched. She clinched and crumpled the papers in her shaking hands.

"Fine." Tobias stood up. "You can leave and take that whore with you."

I never once wanted to hit my brother, but something snapped inside my brain. I growled and charged him. He covered his face, but I didn't care about his face. My fist connected with his stomach. Once he fell forward, clutching his abdomen, and I grabbed his jaw and slammed his head into the wall behind him.

"What is wrong with you?"

He laughed, and blood trickled down his mouth and chin. His mismatched eyes made my stomach turn. He tried to pull at my hand but couldn't pull me off.

"Looks like you won," he laughed. "Go ahead. Kill me."

"I never wanted to win. And I don't want you dead. I just wanted to support you. I'm not an alpha."

"Sure, you are. You have me pinned to a wall."

"You've taken too many pills. That stuff is bad for you."

"It made me strong. I just haven't had enough today."

I slammed him against the wall again. "You're wrong."

His eyes twitched, and I could see the hair on his face lengthen and shorten.

"Tobias," I said, just loud enough for him to hear me. "Are you having problems shifting?"

He growled and tried to move me again.

"Please, let me help you." I knew I looked weak in his eyes, begging to help.

"I don't trust you," he said between clenched teeth.

"Do you trust me?" A high-pitched voice hit my ears.

Tobias relaxed in my grip, his eyes looking past me. "Cindy?"

I turned to look. Rachel stood just in front of her, her eyes on Tobias. Cindy's curly red hair was pulled back into a ponytail. I'd never seen her without make-up and the amount of freckles on her face surprised me.

"Tobias, I'm sorry. What he said is true." Tears fell down her cheeks.

"You smell different," Tobias said. His wolf eye reverted to normal.

I let go of him, and he crumpled to the floor.

Cindy tore past Rachel and kneeled beside him.

"What happened to you?"

"Oliver," he mumbled.

"Oliver, I can't believe you hit a client." She swatted my leg.

"He threw me into a door. And he's not a client. He's my brother."

"Don't give me those excuses." She cupped Tobias's cheek, checking each of the bruises on his face.

Tobias didn't stop staring at her. His shaking hand wrapped around one of her wrists. "Your smell…"

She sighed. "I drank a mixture that changed my scent to that of a shifter. I deceived you. I feel terrible. I've watched you change over the last month, and it hurts my heart."

"No. Your smell." He leaned in and breathed her in.

Rachel pulled me back by my sleeve. "We should leave them," she whispered.

I raised an eyebrow and let her walk me backward.

"You're my mate," Tobias said.

Cindy shrugged. "I don't know what that means."

Rachel pulled me out of the room and marched me into the kitchen. I sat at the table that had four bottles of Brawn-tality sitting in the middle. Coby sat drinking some coffee.

"Want some coffee?" he asked.

"Were you sitting here the entire time I was getting my butt kicked?"

"Nah. I was going to help until you pinned him to the wall."

"You two must never tell anyone that happened." I narrowed my eyes.

"I'd never tell. I know I can kick your ass, and I know Tobias can kick my ass. If this gets out, the others will think I'm weak, too. These pills really had him fucked up." Coby shook one of the bottles.

"Is this all of them?" Rachel asked.

"That's all I can find. I'm sure your dog of a mate might have a better time sniffing them out than me." He grinned at me.

"There is something wrong with you." I stood up and opened a bottle, taking a big sniff. "I'll be right back. Ass."

I heard Rachel laugh as I walked around the house, sniffing out any hidden bottles. I came back with three empty ones.

"How much do you think he's taken over the last month?" Rachel asked, reading the back of the bottle.

"No telling. According to the instructions I read, one bottle is supposed to last for about a month." Coby looked at the wall behind us. "Is it safe to leave the tiniest woman I've ever seen alone with him?"

"Apparently, she is his mate." Rachel grabbed a grocery bag and put all the bottles inside, tying it shut.

"Son of a bitch. That's nuts. The pack is going to have a hard time seeing her around here," Coby said.

"Only if she stays." I shook my head. "She seems to really like him, though. So maybe she'll give it a shot."

Rachel nudged me with her foot. "Come on. Let's go dispose of this somewhere far away from here."

"What about Tobias and Cindy?" I stood up and followed her to the door.

"Coby can stay. The others are still outside. Coby, will you explain to Stone and them what happened?"

It hurt to walk down the stairs now that I'd lost the adrenaline from the fight. The damage from the wall might last for more than a day. The others walked over to us as we exited. Rachel pulled me away as Coby began to fill them in.

"I wonder who let her go into the house," I said to no one.

"I did." Stone appeared beside us.

"What?" I stared at him. Rachel still pulled at me.

"Something about her told me to let her through." He waved and walked back to the group.

Rachel linked her arm through mine. "Are you sore?"

"Of course, I'm sore. He threw me against the wall."

"We can walk slowly. Where do you think we should dispose of this?"

After some thought, I remembered a place I'd taken a client once close to this area. "There is this lovely Italian restaurant in Carrollton."

"Carrollton? That's an hour away."

"Exactly. By the time we get there, it will be close to lunchtime. It's a good distance away to toss the medicine, and we get a nice meal. Do you have somewhere to be today?"

She tapped her chin. "I guess I don't. Alright, heavyweight champ, let's go get the truck."

"I am the champ. I should steal one of his belts."

She laughed. "And hang it on your wall. We can frame it."

"The match of the century, Me versus Tobias. It is the only time I've ever won against him."

"I'm surprised he didn't shift."

I impulsively sucked in a deep breath through my teeth. "About that..."

Chapter 12

Rachel

After disposing of the pills and having an enjoyable lunch, we took the long way back to my house. We walked hand in hand around the territory, talking to the clan members and discussing how Tobias would return to normal within the next week. Oli thought that Tobias's metabolism would kick back in when the steroids started to flush from his system, giving him a shorter withdrawal period.

We turned around at the big oak on the edge of the territory. Oli pulled me close and kissed me under the large branches. He leaned against the trunk, with me in his arms. I looked past him at all the hearts with initials carved all along the trunk of the old oak. I reached past him and touched one of the hearts.

"Do you want to carve our initials in the tree?" I asked. I grinned at him.

His face turned red, and he turned away. "They might already be on there."

"What?" I turned his face toward me. "Where? When?"

My gaze followed the direction he pointed, straight up the tree. "It was a month before I turned eighteen. I didn't like the idea of instantly falling in love with someone or, worse, someone I hated. So, I climbed up to the smallest branch that would hold me, and I carved our initials."

"Why mine?"

"I couldn't think of anyone I'd rather spend my life with. I knew I liked you, but it didn't turn into love until later."

My heart felt full. This man was full of surprises.

"I've seen those initials. I've pretended they were ours for years. When did it turn into love?"

"I realized I love you a year after I left. I was working at that call center and we'd call each other once a week. Even after talking on the phone for work, I wanted to talk to you afterward."

"Didn't you only work there for a year?" I rested my head on his shoulder and watched him.

"Yeah. One night, after spending all day dealing with screaming customers and aloof management, I called you as soon as I stepped into the tiny apartment I had at the time. Only, this time, you didn't answer. I called ten times total over the next hour. They all went to voicemail and I couldn't bring myself to leave you one. My heart ached. All I wanted was to hear your voice, and it wasn't there. That's when I realized I love you."

My heart fluttered as he spoke. Heat washed over my body. I pushed my body flush against his.

"How long I loved you before, I don't know," he continued. "I cried myself to sleep that night, thinking that you'd finally decided to end our friendship."

"I remember that. My parents took away my phone because they caught me skipping school. The next time we talked, you asked if I still wanted to be your friend." I cupped his cheek with my hand. "You've always been my best friend."

He pulled me into a deep kiss. My senses zeroed in on the man in my arms. I loved him so much, I almost forgot to breathe. I suddenly found myself with my back against the tree. I smiled into the kiss. Maybe having sex here under the old oak was one of his fantasies.

His warm hand snuck down my pants and cupped my mound. I tried to look down, but his other hand kept us locked at our lips. Fingers slid further south, rubbing at my nub. I jumped at first contact. He chuckled into the kiss and kept rubbing. His fingers circled my clit, making me pant. I wanted more. My hips gyrated automatically, pressing myself into his palm. His hand slid down lower, slipping a finger into my center, his thumb resting directly on top of my nub. I pressed against him harder.

"You're already so wet," he whispered.

I gasped for breath. "You're not too sore for this?"

Only a few hours ago, he'd been thrown into a wall. He growled, then kissed down my neck while his finger slipped in and out of my vagina. He didn't play fair, so why should I? I unbuckled his belt and unbuttoned his pants, giving myself access to his rock-hard manhood. My hand wrapped around his girth, stroking it slowly. I watched his eyes roll back in his head. His hand slipped out of my center and stopped my fondling. He pushed down my jeans and underwear, exposing me to the elements. If I had known we would end up here, I would have worn a skirt. I couldn't even remember if I owned a skirt. The cool air hit my thighs. He pushed the pants free from one of my legs along with my shoe. The rest of the offending clothing hung around my other ankle. It didn't matter.

I wrapped my legs around his waist. One of his hands slipped under my ass. His hard cock rubbed against my mound. Fingers slid up my side, pushed my bra up off my breast, and pinched my nipple. I gripped and pulled at the back of his shirt. He flicked my nipple again.

"I love to hear your moans," he whispered.

"Was I moaning?" I didn't realize it. I only felt the burning need for him simmering in my core.

He abandoned my breasts to reach between us

and reached around my leg. He forced a condom into my hand.

"Hold this," he said.

He used his free hand to work on his own jeans. I helped him push the fabric down as best I could. His member popped up between our bodies. He rubbed it against me, skin on skin, making me squirm. I wanted him. The teasing drove me crazy. I grabbed his dick and pumped it a few times. He moaned and pulled my hand off.

"Where's the condom?" he asked.

I handed him the object. He pressed me harder into the tree as he fumbled with the wrapper, eventually rolling the condom down his cock. Both of his hands grabbed my ass. He moved me around like I weighed nothing. I felt his shaft at my entrance. He slowly pushed into me and sucked on my mark. Shivers flooded my body and this time I heard myself groan. I clung to his shoulders, his mouth still sucking and nibbling at my mark, as he began pounding into me.

The bark of the tree bit into my back through the shirt, but my legs only squeezed him harder. The trunk propped up my head, my eyes rolled back, and unknown sounds flew out of my mouth. Electricity flowed through my nerve cells.

I dropped my head onto his shoulder. "Harder," I whispered.

He growled into the nape of my neck and

rammed me harder. He lifted his head. "I want to watch you cum."

I looked up at him, my head against the tree. He watched me with those dark brown eyes which I could sink into. I couldn't focus on his face for long. I squeezed my legs harder, desperate to hold on. The pressure built up inside of me and my fingers dung into his back. My pussy pulsed around him as I yelled his name into the forest.

My head dropped just enough for him to kiss me. He moaned into my mouth when he hit his own release. Our foreheads rested against each other's. He continued to sink leisurely in and out of me. We exchanged soft kisses, half naked against the marked tree.

"Was that a fantasy?" I asked.

"Hmm." He rubbed his nose on mine. "Of course."

He pulled out of me and put me safely back on my feet. The tree helped keep me upright. After he took off the condom and pulled up his pants, he methodically redressed me with kisses all the way up both legs. His hands felt warm against my belly, buttoning up my jeans.

He kissed my cheek and pulled me away from the tree and back toward the center of the territory.

"Where are we going?"

"To clean up." He sighed. "Then I need to check on Tobias."

When we approached Tobias's home an hour

later, we found Cindy outside, sitting on the steps. She pulled the legs of her shorts down closer to her knees. The few times I saw her, she wore a skirt suit. Today, she showed up in shorts and a ruffled blouse. She did have great taste in clothes, but it felt too cold for shorts.

"Aren't you a little cold?" I asked when she looked up at us.

"I've been so worried about Tobias that I just left my house in whatever I was wearing and drove here." She scoffed. "He doesn't want me to stay."

"Are you kidding?" Oli asked.

"He doesn't want me to see him go through withdrawal." She rolled her eyes. "I can't believe that I don't want to be anywhere else. I usually hate taking care of someone, even if it's just a headache. But I want to stay here with him."

"When did you fall in love with him?" I sat down next to her. "I'm Rachel by the way."

"I remember seeing you around. I'm Cindy." She dropped her head in her hands. "I knew I liked him the second we met, but the love part snuck up on me. He's the reason I tried to get the company to stop pushing Brawn-tality onto shifters. This is all my fault."

"No. He could have said no at any time." Oli smiled at her and sat down next to me. "And you're his mate. Did he explain all that to you?"

"No. Coby and a man named Stone did. Tobias

fell asleep on my lap at some point. He looks terrible. Did you do all that damage to his face?" She reached across me and poked Oli.

"Ouch." He rubbed his arm. "I guess you didn't see his ribs then."

"Are you kidding?" She tried to swat at him again, but I stopped her.

"He threw Oliver into the door, so they are pretty much even," I said. "Besides, it looks worse than it is. As soon as the medicine leaves his system, he should start healing faster."

"Do y'all really heal faster?"

"We do." I smiled at her. "And I think you should go back in there and demand that he let you stay."

"When do you have to go back to work?" Oli asked.

"Monday. Tomorrow. You?"

"The same, I guess. Though I plan to have a long meeting with Arthur and Mac, then put in my two-week notice. I told them I'd be back Wednesday, but I want to get this over with. I'm sure they won't want a shifter around once they find out."

"You're going to tell them?" I grasped his arm, eyes wide.

"Yeah. They know about shifters. I think it will be a good experience for them to understand how similar we are to each other."

I rubbed his back. My stomach turned. I couldn't imagine telling a bunch of humans. I turned to Cindy. She looked back at the door.

Oliver stood. "I'll be right back."

Chapter 13

Oliver

The house was quiet when I walked inside. Someone cleaned up after our brawl. I hoped Cindy made Tobias do it.

I made my way into the kitchen. Tobias sat with his forehead on the table, and Coby sat across from him, shaking his head.

I sat with them.

"What are you doing here?" Tobias said, lifting his head.

I shrugged. "Don't you think we should talk?"

"Ugh." He put his head down again.

"Cindy's a good person. Let her help you." I leaned back in the chair. "She's still here. Outside on the steps. She doesn't want to leave."

"I don't want her to see me like this," Tobias mumbled into the table.

"She's your mate, right?" Coby asked.

Tobias lifted his head and glared at him.

"She's going to see you in much worse situations down the line. Might as well let her know what she's getting into." Coby reached over to the counter, grabbed a banana, and started eating it.

"Fine. I'll think about it." Tobias looked over at me. "What are you going to do? Do you want to stay?"

"Would you let me stay?" I raised an eyebrow.

"I don't want to. I still think we should fight for it."

"Well, I just kicked your ass," I smirked.

Coby laughed and banged his hand on the table. "You really won that fight."

"Fine," Tobias yelled. "You want the clan?"

I tried not to laugh. I really did, but it came sputtering out. "Hell no. I absolutely do not want the clan."

He glared at me, and his lip twitched.

"Tobias, you are surprisingly calm. You can't have detoxed that fast." I looked between Tobias and Coby for an answer.

"I think it's Cindy." Coby tossed the banana peel in the trash can. "It's keeping Mr. Grumpy Pants at bay."

"What the fuck did you call me?" Tobias stood up and growled.

"You know he's teasing. Sit down."

I could tell he didn't want to sit down but did it anyway. Tobias looked up at the ceiling. It gave me a good view of the damage to his face. Dried blood filled his nose, and I saw the outline of my handprint around his jaw. I wondered if it would be our last fight. He moved and looked directly at me.

"You can stay," Tobias said. "But only because your mate lives here."

"What if she'd rather leave?"

"Then she can leave. I've never forced anyone to stay." He sat back in his chair. "Oh god. I need to apologize to a lot of people."

Coby laughed again, and his head dropped to the table. "Are you just now remembering some of the stuff you did?"

"It's all so hazy. This moment is hazy."

"You'll be fine." I stood up and held out my hand to him. "I need to leave tomorrow. Got to get back to work and properly shut down their plan to make money off of shifters."

He shook my hand. "You coming back?"

"Yeah."

It felt nice to have Tobias show me a genuine smile. Maybe the two of us would mend the bridge between us. "I'll send Cindy in. She may be small, but she's a firecracker. Don't underestimate your mate."

~

Tobias

I rubbed my face with my hands and, again, remembered how much it hurt. The front door opened and light steps followed. My head rested on the table. I told her I didn't want her to see me like this.

I heard the shuffling of paper in the other room. I looked over at Coby who gave me a ridiculously enormous grin. I itched to punch him in the face. I already wanted to take another dose of Brawn-tality, but Oliver took it hours ago. I couldn't believe how addicted I was to it. Thinking about it made me want to sink into a hole.

Cindy walked into the kitchen, looking through a stack of paper. She looked up at me with a soft smile. "Is anyone sitting here?"

I sighed and shook my head. She sat down and continued to look through the papers.

Coby stood up and nodded at me. "I need to get out of here. I'm sure Abby is looking for me."

I glared at him. Abby knew exactly where he was, the liar. I looked back at Cindy. A lone tear traveled down her face.

She looked up at me. "I'm so sorry. I didn't know any of this. They gave me doctored documents. I feel like such a fool. I never meant to hurt you."

"All is forgiven. But you need to leave." My leg shook under the table and my heartbeat felt erratic. I clutched my hands in to fists. "It's not safe to be around me."

She reached over and tucked my hair behind my ear. "I'll leave tomorrow. I'm staying for now. It's too cold outside to wait."

"No, you should leave the territory."

She sighed and set down the papers. "I might not understand the whole mates thing, but it seems like I should stay. At least for a bit."

"It's complicated," I whispered.

She laughed. "Of course it is. But I'll understand it better if you talk to me."

I stared at her. Her lovely freckles, the red hair, and her adorable nose that turned up right at the tip mesmerized me. I wanted her to stay. I wanted to hold her tight. The urge to scream and throw shit at the walls lessened with her around. My wolf wanted to shift and lay at her feet or place his head in her lap.

"Don't you want me to stay?" she asked.

"I never want you to leave."

She placed her small hand over mine. "I'm sure Oliver told you that I came here because of my job. But the first time I saw you, I thought you were the most handsome man I'd ever seen. And you gave me that smile. When I found out you were the person I needed to talk to, I couldn't believe my luck."

"And you knew we were shifters. You weren't

afraid?"

"I was terrified and excited. But I wanted to get to know you."

"Are you scared now?" I placed my other hand on top of hers.

"I'm scared you'll turn me away again. I know the next few weeks will be rough. But I want to be here to help."

"What about your job?"

"You think I'm going to keep working for that company?" She laughed. "I need to go back tomorrow and put in my resignation, but I can find a new job. One closer to here."

My heart felt light, and I grinned my first genuine grin in a month. "You want to live here?"

"Well, not here. I'll find a place close by."

My smile faltered. "But eventually?"

She pulled her hand free and put both hands on my face. "I want to see where this goes. I can't promise much, but I want to give us a chance."

I kissed the palm of her hand. "I'll take it."

Chapter 14

Rachel

I woke up the next morning to an empty bed. My bear sniffed all around the sheets. They still smelled like him. I rushed to check the kitchen but fell off of the bed. I shifted back into a human and rushed around the house naked. I couldn't find the bag he had brought, and his shoes were gone.

My heart was pounding as I stood in the doorway between the living room and kitchen. A piece of paper on the table caught my eye. It was a note from Oli. It read:

Dear Rachel,

I left early this morning with Cindy. You looked so sweet sleeping. I couldn't wake you. Once I finish at the office, I'll come back. I'll always come back, no matter what. Wait for me.

I love you – Oliver

"That idiot," I said to the empty room. We avoided the stupidest conversation. Did he really think I wanted to stay here? I marched into the bedroom and sent a quick message to Uncle Eddie at the diner. Then I got dressed and started to pack.

~

Oliver

I stared across the table at both Arthur and Mac. Both looked unhappy.

"It is unprecedented for a sales rep to call his bosses into a meeting," Arthur said while poking the table with his index finger.

"Come now, Arthur." Mac placed his hand on Arthur's arm. "It must be important for our top sales representative to ask for this meeting."

Arthur sat back in a huff.

I looked between the two men. "You will end the initiative to promote Brawn-tality to the shifter community."

Arthur laughed. "You must be kidding. Why on earth would we do that?"

"The pills cause drastic side effects in shifters that could cause irreparable damage to shifter groups and humans alike." I kept my voice as even as I could.

"There is no basis for that." Author rolled his

eyes.

"There are also no official studies done, which makes this company look bad." I frowned. "The company also hid the amount of anabolic steroids in the pills."

Mac sat up and stared at Arthur. Arthur stood and used the angle to stare down at me.

"Where did you pull that information from? You aren't qualified to have it."

"So, it's true?" Mac asked.

"It is true. Steroids come with a long list of side effects on humans, which increase when taken by shifters. And the company suggested that shifters should take a larger dose of Brawn-tality. It's created a few problems." My temper started to rise, but I had to squash it down.

"Where is this all coming from, Oliver? Are you upset that we offered the initial program development to Cindy?" Arthur gave his best business laugh.

My wolf came forward after I stood up. I knew my eyes would change. I looked Arthur straight in the eyes. He backed up and gripped Mac on the shoulder.

"Not only did you send Cindy into a dangerous situation, but you also handed shifters a product you knew would cause problems. All for money. You caused problems for the clan I grew up in. You caused problems for my brother." I heard my voice become deeper and gruff as I spoke.

"Holy shit, Oliver," Mac said. "You're a shifter?"

"Please don't eat me," Arthur said.

I smiled at the two men. "If I wanted to eat you, you'd be dead by now. Now, you will end the Brawntality/Shifter initiative, or I will release the actual ingredients of the supplement to the public and the FDA. We all know the FDA does not regulate supplements, but they regulate the use of steroids. How much money are you prepared to lose?"

"What do you want?" Arthur said between his teeth.

"Stay away from shifters." I stood and pulled an envelope out of my inner blazer pocket and placed it on the table. "Here is my two weeks' notice."

"Now, Oliver, don't do anything you'll regret." Mac stood up. "You're the best in sales. And now we know you're a shifter; we could learn from your perspective."

Arthur tugged on Mac's arm. "Do you really want to work with a shifter?" he whispered.

"We've worked with him for over five years. How's it different now?"

"Fool." Arthur let go of Mac. "Oliver, we can sue you if you release confidential information."

"I never signed an agreement regarding Brawntality."

"We can tell the other pharmaceutical companies that you're a shifter."

I smiled at him and turned to leave. "Go ahead," I called out over my shoulder.

My shoulders felt light on the way back to my office. I needed to pack up my personal belongings. Once Arthur got over the shock, he wouldn't let me stick around for two weeks. I talked to my contact over at Dunnam Graham today. I had an interview lined up for Wednesday. Now I just needed to grab my things and get out. I could email my clients from home.

Cindy knocked on the door as I put the last of my personal effects in a small box.

"You been kicked out yet?" She leaned against the door frame.

"No. I handed in my notice. I'm still waiting for security to show up."

"They are scrambling a bit at the moment." She clicked her tongue.

"What do you mean?"

"I also gave them my two weeks' notice."

"What? Why?"

She laughed. "That's a stupid question. I can't work at a place that ignores my concerns about a product they want me to sell. Plus, I'm not going to live in the area much longer."

"Are you moving in with Tobias?"

"No. I'll move to a place close by. I can't jump in head first."

"But you love him?"

"I do. I also need time to adjust to shifters and a new relationship."

"I give you three months until you move in. In a

year, you'll officially be my sister-in-law." I waggled my eyebrows.

"Are you taking bets?" She walked over and poked me in the arm.

"I wasn't, but I might start."

"You're the worst brother-in-law."

"Probably." I smiled down at her. "Well, I gotta go. I have quite a drive ahead of me."

"Let me know if they tell you not to come back tomorrow."

I walked out of the office and nodded at Mac, who passed me down the hall.

"Cindy, were you in there with him by yourself?" I heard Mac say.

"Yes."

"Do you know that he's a shifter?"

Her sigh traveled down the hall. "Yeah. It doesn't matter though. I spent a month pitching supplements to shifters."

I turned the corner out of earshot of the rest of their conversation.

~

Oliver

On my way home, Arthur called me as I predicted. He informed me that they could not accept the two weeks' notice and that I would be terminated immediately. They didn't want me to steal company secrets. I thanked him for his time and hung up. I considered calling Mac but decided against it for the time being.

I saw her truck in my driveway before I could see my house. Over the last few hours, I'd sent several text messages to her, but she didn't reply. Now I knew why. I pulled in beside her and jumped out of the car. I planned on returning to the Flint River Clan this afternoon, so I didn't know why she drove all the way here. At the moment, I didn't care.

I rushed through the front door, slammed it shut, and searched the house. I found Rachel in the backyard, walking barefoot in the grass.

"Rachel," I panted.

She turned and blinded me with her smile. "Welcome home."

I picked her up and spun her around. "What are you doing here?"

She wrapped her legs around my waist. "You said you'd catch me if I jumped, right?"

"You want to live here?"

"I want to be with you. And your place is close to the pastry school. I can get a job at any diner while I study."

I leaned in and rested my forehead on hers. "I just walked away from my job."

"I have savings."

I smiled. "Me, too. And a job interview on Wednesday."

"Good. Then I'm staying." She gave me a quick

kiss.

"What about Eddie and the diner?"

"I told him. He wished me luck. Said to tell you not to be stupid."

I laughed. "So, you really want to live here?"

"Of course. I've already hung up my clothes in the closet."

I pulled her into a deep kiss. "What do you want to do to celebrate?"

Her eyes sparkled. "We can start by taking advantage of these extra tall privacy fences."

"I like how you think."

Epilogue(s)

Not All Beds are Created Equal

Rachel

I woke up the next morning curled next to my lovely wolf mate. Oliver decided to try my method of shifting in the middle of the night for a better night's sleep. My bear nuzzled into his warm neck. He slept through it.

I chuckled to myself. Snuggling closer, I licked his nose. His paw reached up and covered his snout. He looked so cute. I rolled over on my head to watch him from a new angle. My bear really liked him. She couldn't wait for the next time we could roam the preserve behind his house. We'd only had time to go once in this first week of cohabitation.

We planned to drive down to the clan today to

pick up some of my things. I wanted to move all at once, but Oliver wanted to move one room at a time. Today, we wanted to move my kitchen. It contained my favorite things. I'd also pick up more clothes.

The last two days, I cleaned out his cabinets of duplicate items, making a list of what to bring based on the quality of his current kitchen versus my own. A few of his items were better than my own. He also lacked a number of utensils and gadgets I used on a regular basis.

He gave me free rein in the kitchen and helped about 80% of the time. The other 20% he spent trying to seduce me into bed or to have sex on the kitchen floor. I never complained. I'd never admit it to him, but I initiated a good portion of our kitchen escapades with just a sultry look.

But right now, I wanted to see what exactly I could do to my sleeping wolf before he'd wake up.

I jumped off the bed and walked around the room. His home had a concrete slab, so walking around didn't exactly make noise, especially in the carpeted room. Next, I grabbed the comforter with my mouth and dragged it off of him. Oli slept soundly.

I sighed and jumped back onto the bed, snuggling close. I tried to use our mind link to wake him up. I couldn't even tell if he was dreaming. His head turned away from me and I huffed into the back of his head. I stretched, then lay on my side, looking at my fluffy wolf. My paws reached up to the headboard, and I rolled onto my back and off the bed.

My bear and I stared up at the ceiling. My heart pounded from the adrenaline and my furry cheeks felt warm. Over the edge of the bed popped a wolf's head that looked down at me on the floor.

Oliver shifted back; his eyes wide with a frown. "Are you okay?"

I closed my eyes and covered my face with a paw.

"Are you blushing? As a bear?"

I could hear the laughter in his voice. Then his hands scratched my belly. I sighed and shifted, showing a huge frown with a big lip stuck out.

"My poor pouty bear." He pulled me back onto the bed with ease.

I curled into his arms. "The bed's too small," I said in my smallest voice.

"Too small?" He nuzzled the top of my head. "Are you sure that's the reason you fell?"

"Of course. This could never happen if we were in my bed."

He laughed. "Do you want to bring your bed up here? There's room for a king. I'm not married to this bed."

I cocked my head to the side and looked at him. "You wouldn't mind?"

"Of course not. Whatever you need or want, we will make it work." He paused and squinted. "Well, within reason."

"What's unreasonable?"

"Covering the walls with papier-mâché.

Decorating with beer cans. Hamburger bed. Playing 'Cotton Eye Joe' while we make love." He clicked his tongue. "I probably have more."

"I'm sad about the last one." I tried to keep a straight face, but he began to tickle me.

Once we calmed down, he pulled me close and kissed my nose. "We can pick up the bed this weekend. I'll call to see if we can rent a truck."

~

Rachel

I considered the first trip to move stuff a success. My bed, now our bed, stood in the bedroom. It didn't quite match the dark wood of the rest of his furniture, but only those who looked hard would notice.

We unpacked the kitchen in no time. His interview the week before landed him the job at Dunnam Graham and he planned to start next week. Instead of organizing the house for my next trip home, I decided I'd just move the rest of my clothes and my crochet supplies.

We spent that week cuddling instead. And making love, roaming the preserve, and adjusting to each other. I woke up that Friday, much as I had the week before. My love slept in his wolf form as I stared at him. I licked his nose, hoping to see his eyes pop open. He didn't stir. With a sigh, I stretched in my spot and rolled onto my back, only to fall off the bed again.

A wolf's head peeked over the side, down at me again, then shifted. Oli howled with laughter, laying down on the bed, clutching his stomach. I shifted and stood.

"I can't believe you're laughing at me."

He waved his hand in front of his face. Tears ran down his cheeks. His head turned red from laughing so hard.

My lip twitched. I couldn't hold it in. I tackled Oli on the bed and laughed with him. He kissed me through the laughs.

"I'm so happy."

~

Rachel fell off that same bed at least once a year for the rest of their lives.

Fun with Hats

Oliver

Fall faded into Winter, where I celebrated my first holiday with my brother in nine years. My best present finished moving all her stuff into my home, making it our home. That January, she started pastry school. Working at Dunnam Graham wasn't much different from working at Landry & Caddel, especially when Mac Stephenson joined our team. He left soon after Cindy and I. He told me later that he enjoyed working with me. As a homosexual, he'd experienced discrimination, and he didn't want to continue to work with Arthur after hearing listening to his rant regarding shifters. Our friendship grew from there and soon he and his husband even moved into the same subdivision.

Winter leaped into spring. The last few weekends, I spent my days out in my garden, redesigning the succulent garden. I potted most of the succulents to sell or give away. I only needed a few with the new plan.

With the help of my tools and a few trips to the hardware store, I put together a tiered box where the succulent garden once sat. After installing the box, I filled it up with dirt and let it settle for a week. After a lengthy visit to the local nursery, I had everything I needed to complete a flourishing herb garden. Between the three tiers, we would grow sage, oregano, rosemary, basil, thyme, parsley, dill, and mint.

While I worked, I often had an admirer lounging in a chair with a glass of tea. Whenever I asked her to join me, she said, "Oh, I'm enjoying the view."

More often than not, I'd roll my eyes and continue. One warm Saturday, I began planting the top tier, now that I fully set the garden up. My admirer never joined me at her post as supervisor.

Bent down on my knees, the sun beat down on my back. It felt nice to walk outside without a chill in the air. My gloved hands made tiny wells in the dirt of where each seedling would go. I would finish the herb garden this afternoon, then my lovely chef could put fresh ingredients into her breads and other pastries.

I thought about how she looked kneading dough on the counters. She put her entire body into it. The muscles in her arms flexed. She'd give a little grunt, and her tits jiggled. I think I understood why she liked to watch me garden.

Lost in my own thoughts, I felt arms snake around my waist.

Rachel kissed me on the cheek. "Are you ready to take a break?"

"Let me finish planting this seedling." I smiled.

"Hmm." She licked my face.

"Are you trying to distract me?"

"Um hmm." Her hands rubbed up and down my chest.

"I won't be able to play if you don't let me plant this oregano."

She kissed and sucked on my neck, obviously ignoring my words. It already riled my wolf up inside. He wanted to know what was so important about oregano anyway, especially since our mate wanted our attention.

Focus. I needed to focus. I couldn't always give into her. I took a few deep breaths and tried to not crush the plant in my hand.

Her warm hands slid into the waistband of my pants. She chuckled in my ear when she found me already hard. Her fingers wrapped around my stiff length and stroked me. I moaned. I'd have to abandon my efforts to garden for the next few hours.

The seedling fell to the dirt, and I leaned against the top of the three-tiered box. I pulled off my gloves and turned toward her. She smiled a devilish grin. Her hand was still down my pants, making it hard to think, but I knew she had something different planned. She pulled us both up to stand when I attempted to push her back on the soft grass.

Our faces almost touched. "I have a little something for you," she said and gave me a quick peck on the lips.

"Is that right?" I put my hands on her waist, running them up her sides.

Her grin showed all her teeth, and she nodded. My shorts slipped off me and landed on the ground. She pulled my aching cock out of my underwear. Her eyes lazily looked down. I continued to watch her face. How she bit her bottom lip looked adorable.

Her finger rubbed over the tip of my penis, followed by the feeling of something being slipped over the head. Whatever she placed there didn't feel bad, but didn't feel great either.

She immediately started giggling. I really didn't want to look down at the item she placed on my dick.

"You look so serious," she said through her laughter.

I took a deep breath and looked down to see a tiny, wide-brimmed hat on my cock. "Why does my penis have a hat?"

"Well, you refuse to garden while naked. I thought I'd get you a few hats to encourage you to take off your clothes."

My eyes widened. "How many hats?"

"That is on a need-to-know basis." She kneeled

down in front of me, keeping her hand wrapped around my length.

I smiled down at her. I'd wear all the hats if it meant getting a blow job. She peered at my penis from the left and right.

"I know what this needs." She stuck her hand in her pocket and pulled out a permanent marker. She clicked the button on the end of the retractable pen and moved toward my behatted dick.

"No, you don't." I grabbed her hands and pulled away from her.

"It needs a little face to go with the hat."

"It absolutely does not need a face. This isn't penis cosplay time."

She raised an eyebrow. "When is penis cosplay time?"

"When is vagina cosplay time?"

She narrowed her eyes. "That might be a little uncomfortable."

"You don't think this isn't uncomfortable?" My now flaccid cock hung down, surprisingly the hat didn't fall off.

"How about boob cosplay and penis cosplay?" she asked with doe-like eyes.

I pulled her close. "How can I say no to that?"

A Little Story about Slapping

Rachel

I loved pastry school. I loved the baking classes, the other students, and I even enjoyed the general education courses. But by the end of the day, I felt exhausted. I wanted nothing more than to curl up with Oliver. After almost six months of living together, life couldn't be better.

After a late day at school, I pulled into the driveway and could smell someone grilling in their backyard. I hoped the smells came from my house. The scent through the door confirmed my hopes. That delicious aroma of steak definitely came from our backyard. I threw my bag on the couch and walked into the kitchen.

One nice plump ass greeted me. Oliver was bent over next to the island, giving me one hell of a view. A smirk graced my face.

I had yet to slap his round bottom like he slapped mine in our deepest throes of passion. While I loved the feeling, it seemed a little one sided. I told him that my turn was coming. Now my chance stood just a few feet away.

I licked my lips and tiptoed across the floor. I wanted this to create a loud smack sound. With any luck, he'd have my handprint on his ass for a few days.

My arm pulled back by my side. Two more steps and I'd be close enough to let loose. My hand swung down. A countdown played in my head.

Five.

Four.

Three.

Two.

The backdoor opened. Oliver took one step into the house. In slow motion, I watched his smile turn into a wide-eyed and open-mouthed shock.

It was already too late. I couldn't stop my hand.

One.

My hand connected to the right butt cheek of an unknown man bending over in my kitchen. So many thoughts rushed through my head. Why didn't I smell this person? Who did I just hit? How did I become so unlucky? Would Oliver ever not tease me about this moment? And most importantly, did I really not know what Oliver's ass looked like?

A blonde headed man stood up straight with a yelp. My eyes grew to the size of plates. Mac Stephenson. He'd joined Oli at his new company four months ago. He and his husband moved into the same neighborhood. And today was Friday.

Shit! I'd forgotten about the dinner Oli planned to have with the other couple. I told him this morning I'd pick up wine on the way home. Of course, I'd forgotten about that, too.

Oliver's hand covered his mouth while Mac's spouse, Frank, ran up to him.

"Honey, are you okay?" Frank practically pulled Mac away from me.

"I am so sorry," I said. "I thought…" I couldn't even think of a way to finish that sentence. My face felt hot and Oli stood back, biting his bottom lip while his shoulders shook.

Mac rubbed his bottom and looked up at me. A small tear ran down his face. "That was some slap."

Frank rubbed Mac's bottom as well. "My poor Mac." He narrowed his eyes on me.

Not only was Frank a personal trainer, he also participated in amateur boxing competitions. I never thought I'd fear a human until that moment. He stood half a foot taller than me. His muscles pushed the stretchability of his shirt to the limit on a good day, but now he seemed to swell like a puffer fish. And right now, I wanted to dig a hole and hide.

Oli pulled me into his arms with a chuckle. He

rubbed my back. I peeked over at Mac and Frank.

"I'm really sorry," I said. I'd need to make this up to them, and fast.

Mac gave me a smile. "Besides the bruise I'm sure to have tomorrow, I'm flattered that you think my ass looks as good as Oliver's."

"Have you been checking out Oliver's ass?" Frank glared at his husband.

Mac hugged Frank. "Like you haven't."

Frank deflated a bit and stuck out his lip at Mac. He still glared at me, but it lacked the fire behind it now.

"Okay, everyone outside. The steak's probably burning on the grill." Oli herded the two men outside. Before I could walk out the door, he pulled me back and whispered, "I didn't know you wanted to spank me so bad that you'd mistake anyone's ass for mine?"

"Hush you," I whispered back.

"Or maybe you'd like me to spank you tonight?"

"If anyone's getting spanked, it's you." I poked him in the chest and walked out the door. He followed me out, laughing.

Oliver

A month after my fight with Tobias, he called me unexpectedly. After a rather stilted and strange conversation, I agreed to his request.

After the call, I turned to Rachel, who sat next to me on the couch crocheting. "Tobias wants me to help rebuild Pine's porch."

She raised an eyebrow and smiled. "I bet Cindy put him up to it."

"You think so?"

"Yeah. Seems like something she'd do." She looped yarn around her needle and stuck it through a hole in the pattern.

"Since when do you know Cindy well enough to

make that determination?"

"We talk all the time."

"All the time?" I scrunched up my face and moved close to her cheek.

"Yeah. I gave her my number, so she had someone to call with questions about shifters and clan life."

I kissed her. "I don't deserve you."

"Sure, you do." She grinned. "In exchange, I hear stories about you when y'all worked together."

I groaned.

~

Oliver

The next Saturday, Rachel and I drove to the clan's territory. When we arrived early that morning, Rachel patted my back and said, "Have fun." I did not know where she went after that.

She left me in front of Pine and Fern's house. Half of their bright purple porch laid in piles on the ground. The other half held on for dear life to the front of the pale-yellow house. I found the color combination...interesting.

The unfinished wood door opened over the porch currently dead on the ground and Pine stuck her head out. "Hey, Oliver. Are you going to help your brother?"

"That's the plan."

"Okay. I'll come right out. Gotta leave through the back door." She disappeared inside. Pine and Fern would have to use the back door to come and go, unless they wanted to jump three feet up and down to reach the front door.

Pine appeared beside me and crossed her arms over her chest. "It's a mess."

"It sure is. I can't believe he did this."

"I can't believe he asked you to help." She nudged my shoulder with her own. "I guess his mate is a good influence. I like her at least."

We looked up at the sound of Tobias walking up the driveway with a large toolbox in hand. He nodded his head at us. "Pine. Oliver."

"Well, Tobias. I'll leave this for you and your helper. Let me know when I can start painting." She hugged Tobias and then hopped in her car and drove away.

"I heard you didn't like the color." I smirked at my brother.

He pushed me. "I can't believe you agreed to help. What a pain in the ass."

I laughed, though my shoulders felt tense. "Do you even remember doing this?"

"I remember." He sighed. "I do hate the color, but it's not my house. I never wanted to run this clan like a damned homeowner's association."

"Well, what's the plan? Do we need to get some wood?" I picked up some broken wood off the ground. We couldn't salvage any of this to rebuild the porch.

"Coby's coming back with the wood. Once he gets here, we'll unload it, then load up this scrap into the back of his truck."

I stood back and watched my brother. He didn't look away from me when we talked, but he didn't stare at me longer than necessary. His eyes appeared clear, and he lacked the dark circles under them from the month before. He wore a worn-out pair of jeans and a long sleeve t-shirt covered in stains. I didn't expect him to wear his best outfit to rebuild a porch, but I appreciated the lack of mud. I wondered how much I could tease him before he pushed back.

"Are you feeling better?" I asked.

"Yeah."

"How often do you see Cindy?"

He gave me a side eye. "Almost every day. Why?"

I shrugged. "No reason."

"You stay away from her."

I laughed and pushed him. "Idiot. I think she's gonna be a good influence on you."

A tinge of pink flushed his cheeks. "Let's start moving this wood out of the way and see if we can use the part that's still attached to the house."

He shuffled away and began picking up the scraps. I followed suit.

Hours later, the basic structure of the porch took shape. We needed to nail down the planks for the floor and tack up the lattice skirting. Coby cut the boards to length while Tobias and I nailed them down. The work would move faster if Coby didn't stop to have a snack every half hour.

As Coby shared more about his life over the last nine years, slowly, Tobias and I did the same. The tension in my shoulders decreased as the day progressed. The conversation between the three of us started to sound like it did ten years ago. Tobias told me how he expanded the farm's operations and even sold the jellies, jams, and preserves in stores across ten counties. He couldn't believe that I found a safe place to shift so close to the city and that I was friends with a six-foot-tall squirrel shifter. I told him I'd introduce him if he ever came to visit.

By the end of the day, the porch only lacked railings. We sat on the newly built steps and drank the beer Fern handed us.

"Good work," she said before she floated back inside.

Tobias raised an eyebrow and watched her leave.

"You know they aren't going to tell you 'Thank you', right?" Coby said.

Tobias took a swig of his beer. "Yeah, I know."

"Did they ask you to rebuild it?" I asked.

"No. Cindy suggested I offer since I destroyed it. I didn't realize how much better I would feel physically fixing my mistake." He rubbed his face.

"I'm sure everyone is already talking about it." I clapped him on the back.

"Oh yeah. This is going to help you in the long

run," Coby said. "You've always helped out around here, but doing something like this goes a long way. It's easy to talk. It's not so easy to take action."

"Have you apologized for all the groping?" I looked at him through the small slits in my eyelids.

His shoulders sank. "Yes. All except Rachel. She hasn't been here. The worst was apologizing to Myrtle."

"And why was that the worst?" Coby asked with a huge smile. "You can tell Oliver. Come on."

Tobias shot daggers at Coby with his eyes. "She wouldn't accept my apology unless I let her grab my ass."

"That's amazing." I smiled at him.

"The best part is that Cindy was there. She looked at Tobias and said, 'What are you waiting for? Turn around and stick out your butt.'" Coby's grin reached his ears.

Tobias's face turned red while I clutched my stomach while laughing.

"Alright, you two. Stop laughing or I won't feed either of you dinner."

We both swallowed our hysterics as best we could. Coby hopped in his truck and waved with a promise to see us at dinner.

"You're really cooking for us?" I asked.

"Sure."

We walked in silence toward his house roughly a quarter mile down the road.

"I was wondering," he began. "Would you and Rachel like to have Christmas dinner with me, with us, this year?"

I stopped and turned toward him. He looked into my eyes, then down at the ground. It felt like he was holding his breath.

"You mean that?"

"Yeah. I want you to come."

I smiled. "Then we'll be there."

We continued walking toward his home, the place we both grew up. While I'd driven back and forth to the clan's territory several times over the last few weeks, this moment made me feel like I'd come home.

The Alpha's Alpha

Tobias

It's been two months since Cindy moved to the area and she's stopped by my place almost every night. She found a job consulting with sales and business projects for large firms. Most of her work was over the phone or through online meetings. Some of it required her to drive into Atlanta, but she didn't seem to mind.

Though, I minded. After working at the farm all day, then dealing with any clan business, I wanted nothing more than to hold her. Even though she came most days, it wasn't every day. I wanted her to move in now.

I fretted over the stove, trying to cook something she'd like. Tacos didn't take long, and it was something I cooked successfully. I still felt nervous around her and my wolf prancing around in my head when she was near didn't help.

I walked over to the doorway leading to the living room and peeked around the corner at the front door. Why wasn't she here yet? This entire situation was nerve-wracking. A human mate.

I took a deep breath. I could do this. Just because I always assumed my mate would be a shifter didn't mean anything changed. I walked back to the counter and shredded some cheese. I stared at the cheese piling up. It changed everything.

Cindy didn't feel the pull like I did. Sure, as shifters we could deny our mates. As an alpha, I never planned to do that. Part of the duty my father ingrained in me was to find my mate and produce the next in line. Not everything my dad taught me worked out like I thought, mainly the situation with Oliver. Since I was five-years-old, I thought I'd have to fight Oliver to prove myself as a worthy alpha. Apparently, no one told Oliver.

Being apart from my brother for nine years gave me time to ponder the real duties of an alpha and I questioned how many of our traditions needed to continue. I learned that time moves forward, whether or not we move with it. The issue of tradition versus change divided the elders, and we continued those discussions occasionally.

The front door opened. I dropped what I was doing and rushed to the living room. She walked in wearing a red pants suit with a pale blue button-up blouse. I never knew that a redhead could pull off a red suit.

Compared to shifters, she looked tiny. She stood almost a foot shorter than me. While she looked thin in her suits, I learned they masked her curvy figure. She draped her blazer over the back of the couch, looked up, and smiled at me. That smile melted all my worries.

"Hey, beautiful." I pulled her into a hug, inhaling her scent of blackberries and cinnamon.

She kissed my cheek. "Hello, handsome."

I took her hand and pulled her into the kitchen. "Did you have a good day?"

"I did. I'm working on some interesting projects."

She stopped in the middle of the floor, still holding my hand.

"What's wrong?"

"What are we doing?" She frowned at me.

"Eating dinner?"

"No. What are we doing? I come here every day. We eat. Sometimes cuddle. Is that all? Do you actually like me, or is it all this bond thing?" Her southern accent increased the more she spoke.

My heart pounded in my chest. I thought my biggest fear was claustrophobia, but now I realized it was Cindy leaving for good. My hands felt sweaty and my wolf whined in my head.

"It's both." Had I not made that clear?

"Both?" She frowned.

"Cindy, why don't you sit down and I'll explain." I pulled her to the kitchen table, then turned off all the burners on the stove.

I pulled up a chair beside hers and sat down facing her. "Do you remember the first time we met?"

She nodded. I took her hands in mine and smiled down at her. Light bounced off her unruly hair, making it looked like she wore a red crown.

"The first time I saw you, you were at the farm, walking through the store, looking at the shelves of jellies and jams. I noticed you through the window of the shop. You held yourself with such confidence. I watched as you used your finger to help look at all the names of the products. Half-way through the shelves, you turned and walked away. I panicked, because I thought you were leaving."

She smiled at me. "I was going to get a basket."

"Right. I walked in through the back, hoping to catch you, but you'd already grabbed a basket and started pulling jars off the shelf."

"That's when you started talking to me." She squeezed my hand.

"After that, I couldn't wait to see you again. Even though I thought you were a shifter and that you weren't my mate, I wanted to spend more time with you. Talking to you was easy. It is easy. You're funny and smart and I don't think you're afraid of anything."

"And that's not the bond talking?" She furrowed her brows.

"No. Before, when you disguised your scent, I felt nervous and excited, waiting for you to show up or text me back. I have that same feeling now, but it's more intense."

Her hand reached up to my face and caressed my cheek. Her hand dropped back in to her lap. "Why don't you...pursue anything with me?"

"What do you mean?" Did she just ask why I hadn't initiated sex?

"I've known you three months. The first month was a bit weird at the end. But since then, we've kissed and did some hands stuff, but you've put a stop to going further." Her freckled nose scrunched up. "I wasn't sure if you really liked me or if you felt obligated to, I don't know, keep me."

I grinned at her, trying not to chuckle. "Oh Cindy, I want to fuck you until you're hoarse from screaming my name."

Her hazel eyes dilated, and I felt her shiver through the hand I held.

"The reason I haven't done anything is because I don't know if I'd be able to keep myself from marking you," I said.

"Marking. That's where you leave a scar on me and we are officially together?"

"Yes. I'd leave a permanent indent without breaking the skin. I want you to wait until you are ready. If I break the skin, you'll become a wolf shifter, and that's a different discussion."

"How will you know when I'm ready?"

I cupped her cheek. "You'll tell me."

She narrowed her eyes at me. "That's a rather permanent action. And I don't feel comfortable making that decision if I haven't had sex with you."

"What?" Of all the things she could say, that wasn't one I expected.

"This isn't Edwardian England. I'm an adult and part of growing a relationship is finding out if we are compatible. Sexually."

I swallowed and my dick swelled. "Oh."

She grinned up at me, then moved to straddle my lap. She wrapped her arms around my neck and kissed my nose. "There are a few things we can try if you are worried about marking me."

"What, like oral sex?"

"Yes. That's one option. Another is putting a gag on you."

"A gag? On me?" I never considered the possibility, but I liked the sound of it.

She leaned close and licked the side of my mouth. "Yeah. It might be fun stepping away from being in charge for a little while."

"A little while? How long is a little while?"

She gyrated in my lap, obviously attuned to my stiff member. "Depends on how long you can last."

My hands gripped her bottom. "That sounds like a good plan. Like something I'd be willing to try."

She leaned forward and kissed me. Her tongue danced with mine instantly. The slow, methodical kiss felt like heaven and torture all at once. I massaged her ass while her fingers gripped my hair. My hands roamed up her back and pulled her shirt out of her pants. Her skin felt like silk on my hands. The more skin I touched, the more desperate the kiss became. Her hands released my hair and squeezed my shoulders.

She kissed across my cheek to my ear, nibbling on the lobe. I never knew my ear was an erogenous zone. The sensation zipped straight down to my cock, making it twitch. She pulled off my shirt and ran her fingers through my chest hair.

While her hands roamed my upper body, I unbuttoned her blouse. I slid it off her shoulders and down her arms. Freckles dotted her shoulders and all down her torso. I wanted to kiss each one. Her bosom nearly spilled out of her bra. I hated to see her breast held down by an unruly contraption.

With a flick of my fingers, her bra few open in the back. I looped my finger around the fabric between her cleavage and pulled the offending article off her. I stared at her freed tits. The freckles matched the color of her nipples. My hands gravitated toward them, wanting to see her reaction when I touched her nips.

Her breast felt heavy in my hand. I squeezed it and ran my thumb over the nipple. Her quick intake of breath sounded like a win. I did it again, and she squirmed in my lap. I licked my lips and took her taunt nipple into my mouth.

She moaned. My other hand slipped under her waistband and grabbed her ass. Was she even wearing underwear? Her hands gripped my head while I sucked on her beautiful breast.

The sound of the front door opening startled both of us. I looked up and pulled her close to me.

"Get out," I yelled. "Whatever it is, it can wait."

"Okay," Coby said. He hadn't made it to the kitchen.

I heard him turn and walk away. "I'll lock it behind me," he said, then closed the door. I listened to his footsteps down the stairs.

Cindy looked at me with a huge grin on her face. She climbed off me and pulled me up. I let her pull me into my bedroom, where she pushed me down on the bed and climbed over me.

"Are you always so aggressive in the bedroom?" I asked, mesmerized by the swing of her breasts.

"Always. I hope you don't mind following my lead. I've been wanting to do this for weeks." She leaned down and kissed me like we hadn't seen each other for years. It felt like she touched me everywhere all at once. I could barely keep up.

She kissed down my neck and down my chest and stomach. "I always thought an actual six pack was a myth."

She licked each one before stopping at my belt. With deft fingers, she unbuckled my belt and undid my pants faster than I thought possible. She slid her hands inside my underwear and rubbed the underside of my stiff dick.

"So, alpha, what do you think we can use for a gag?"

I could hardly think. "I think…I think there's a bandana in a drawer." I pointed the best I could toward the top drawer of my dresser.

She pulled down my underwear and kissed the head of my penis, then slipped off me to rummage through the drawer. She came back and opened the nightstand. As she pulled out condoms, she raised an eyebrow.

"I like a man who's prepared." Her soft hand caressed my face, then tied the bandana around me, making it hard to bite down.

I leaned over and unbuttoned her slacks and watched them fall to the floor. I moaned when I saw her wearing only a thong. I looped a finger around the sting of a waistband and tugged them down. She stepped out of them. She stuck her ass in my face as she pushed down my pants. I palmed her rear with both hands. I helped kick off my remaining clothes and pulled her back onto the bed.

I leaned back on the headboard and laid her on top of me, her back to my front. I reached around and ran my hand down her front to her smooth mouth. She arched her back when I touched her sensitive clit, but I wanted something more. I wanted to know exactly how wet she was.

My fingers slipped inside her with ease. My control wavered. Maybe I could get her to sit on my face first. I pulled down my makeshift gag.

"Baby, come sit on my face," I whispered. I added another finger into her warm center and my other hand pinched a nipple.

"Not today." She pulled my hand away from her dripping pussy.

She rolled over, straddled my waist, and leaned down so her lips touched my earlobe. "Right now, I want to ride you like a cowgirl." Her southern accent came out, hitting all the right notes. She slipped the bandana over my mouth again.

"I'll go slow, but if it's too much, you need to pat me on the arm in quick succession since you're gagged. Now stay still."

She moved down my body, lightly scraping my skin with her nails. Her eyes stared at my cock. She smiled and licked it from base to tip. Her mouth slipped over the head and she almost swallowed me whole. I shivered. No one had even attempted to deep throat me before. Her head bobbed up and down, and I felt fingers fondle my balls.

I placed my hand on her head, and her nails dug into my testicles. I moved my hand off her head, and the nails subsided. With wide eyes, I looked down at her still sucking my dick. She looked at me through her lashes and winked before she moved her head faster.

She brought me right to the edge, then backed

off. Her hand slowly stroked me while she licked all around the head.

She grabbed a condom and slipped it on. Her leisurely crawl up my body drove me insane. I wanted to suck her nipples while she rode me. I wanted to kiss her while I pounded her from behind. And I wanted to eat that pussy of hers until she passed out from pleasure.

She grabbed one of my hands and sucked on my thumb. Her other hand was flat against my chest, burning a hole in me. She came off my thumb with a loud pop and she leaned forward and licked my neck.

Her body hovered over mine, then she lined me up and slid herself over me. I grabbed her hips and pushed her all the way down. I moaned. She felt so wet and so tight. My self-restraint wouldn't last much longer.

She gasped. Her chest rose and fell as her breaths quickened. She placed her hands on my stomach for support, then glided herself around my dick. My hands tightened around her hips, frantic to continue.

She looked down at me and covered my hands with her own. "Next time, you won't be able to touch until I say you can." She cocked her head to the side. "Do you understand?"

I nodded. The thought of giving her complete control sent chills through my body. It sounded like delicious torture. Her body moved again, bringing me back to the present. She leaned forward, her hands on my shoulders, riding me. I let her set the pace while I caressed her breast and flicked each tip.

She reacted to each twist and tug. Her pussy squeezed around me like she didn't want to let me go. She grabbed my hands and pulled them together on my chest.

"No more touching," she said with a wink.

Her hands pressed down on my wrist as she sped up. I matched her speed with my thrusts and watched her breast jiggle before my eyes. Red hair fell loose from its confines, waving wildly all around. Her head bent back the faster she impaled herself on my cock. I'd never felt so turned on. This is where I wanted her for the rest of our lives, right here riding my dick. If only I could mark her. I wanted to see my imprint on her freckled shoulder. I wanted her to mark me right on the neck, where everyone could see.

My fingers itched to touch her, but I couldn't deny how turned on I felt from just feeling her ride me and watching her bounce. Sweat rolled down her neck and in between her breast. Her sweet smell of blackberries and cinnamon filled the room.

The pressure built up in my groin. She moved faster and squeezed around my dick more, as if she knew. Her nails bit into my arms, her breasts bounced, and she pulsed around me, falling into her bliss. Her cunt clinched around my dick as she shattered and I spilled over with her.

Her grip on my arms lessened and she released me from her hold. She looked down at me with her bright hazel eyes while she slowly pumped me dry. Those eyes came closer to me as she laid on my chest.

"Well, that's something I'd like to do again." She smiled and pulled my gag off.

"You can do that any time you want." I wrapped my arms around her.

"Did you like me having control?"

"More than I thought I would," I said.

"Mind if I tie you up next time?"

My dick twitched. The thought brought a smile to my face. "You going to tie me up and sit on my face?"

"There's an idea. I like how you think, my alpha." She smirked.

I pulled her into a slow kiss. "I think you'll find that you are my alpha, sweetheart."

"Is that so? I'm the alpha's alpha?"

I laughed. I suppose she was the alpha's alpha. Just as long as she wasn't anyone else's alpha.

She propped her head up on her hand, her elbow on my chest. "How do you feel about being spanked?"

A month later, she moved onto clan territory and into my...our house. After six months, I asked Cindy to take over the advertising and business side of Old Flint Farm. A month after that, I proposed.

We got married the following spring. That night, we marked each other.

If you enjoyed my book...

Don't forget to check out the others in the Corporate Shifter collection.

Return to Blackcreek by Quell T. Fox -

https://books2read.com/returntoblackcreek

Bear With Me by TJ Bell -

https://www.amazon.com/dp/B0BGKGXZQR

Challenging the Alpha by Lilly Rayman -

http://books2read.com/ChallengingTheAlpha

Unexpected Mate by Morgan Meyer -

https://www.amazon.com/dp/B0BGVBY6M7

Claiming Emma by Leeah Taylor -

https://www.amazon.com/dp/B0BGK9LYVD

Also by Lucille Yates

A Bite of Magic Saga

The Wolf's Bite
The Witch's Complement
The Wolf's Return
The Wolf's Song

Did you enjoy this book?

Please review and visit Lucille's website for updates, sign up for her newsletter, and learn how to find her across social media.

www.lucilleyateswrites.com

About the Author

Lucille Yates writes paranormal romance and urban fantasy stories. They feature headstrong women, complicated men, and sizzling chemistry.

Lucille enjoys writing the stories that are constantly playing like a movie in her head. She is excited that others will now enjoy them as much as she does.

When she is not writing, she is reading, playing with her eight-year-old son, watching videos, or playing games. She lives outside of Savannah, GA with her husband, son, and three cats.